Merry Christmas
Paco Alvarez

Merry Christmas Paco Alvarez

John Raab

authorHOUSE®

AuthorHouse™ LLC
1663 Liberty Drive
Bloomington, IN 47403
www.authorhouse.com
Phone: 1-800-839-8640

Published by AuthorHouse   07/11/2013

ISBN: 978-1-4817-6580-0 (sc)
ISBN: 978-1-4817-6581-7 (e)

Library of Congress Control Number: 2013910982

Any people depicted in stock imagery provided by Thinkstock are models, and such images are being used for illustrative purposes only.
Certain stock imagery © Thinkstock.

This book is printed on acid-free paper.

Chapter One

The weatherman will tell you the coldest day of the year in Indiana is in the middle of January, typically about thirty days after the shortest sunlight day of the year, but he is mistaken. He may be technically correct, the coldest temperature of the year is in mid-January, but the coldest day of the year comes in November, or sometimes late October. It happens when you least expect it, and it is a brisk awakening.

The day starts out deceitfully comfortable, only cool enough for a sweater or windbreaker, but by the time you get out of school, or off from work, and you open the door to go to your transportation you are blasted by a frigid wind, and you are pelted with ice-cold raindrops or sleet, and your sweater gets soaked and clings to your suddenly brittle skin, and the goose bumps pop out on your arms and legs, and your chin tries to make you stutter out a breathy two-note song. That is the coldest day of the year; because it is the day you feel the coldest.

In 1962 the coldest day came in late November. I had suffered through another grueling seven hours with Sister Boniface, (in those days nuns took saints' names as their own and we never learned their given name or identity) in room 4B at Our Lady of the Golden Flower School. That day I was forced to stay in the classroom during recess, my desk positioned in the dreaded spot next to Sister Boniface, and, according to her, it would stay there until my penmanship improved. I spent those interminable recess minutes making those mindless horizontal tornadic scrawls dictated by the almighty Palmer Method to Better Penmanship. I knew in my mind, and still know to this day, that my penmanship would not, and will not, improve; but I instinctively knew it could not be done. God knows I tried and tried and tried to make my handwriting pretty, because I was desperate to avoid Sister Boniface's scrutiny. She would put a semi-transparent sample page of what the pre-lettering scribbles should look over my work and compare the two. Of course mine always looked like the doctor's hand. I was in fourth grade and I had yet to progress to the lettering portion of the Palmer Method.

So focused was I on the Palmer Method drills that I did not notice the purple lips or dripping noses of my classmates when they returned from the playground, so I was not yet aware that it was the coldest day. My thoughts were deeply focused on penmanship and finding a way out of sitting next to Sister Boniface.

The dismissal bell rang at 3:05 as it did every day, but we did not leap to exit as one might expect. We waited for Sister Boniface to give us the signal to rise and say our last prayer of the day. We recited our prayer and marched out silently, in single file, ladies first, to the door of our classroom. Once in the hallway those who were wise enough to wear coats retrieved them from the once-shiny-brass, but now brown, tarnished, three-pronged hooks and donned them. I, ignorant of the weather, (and so much else) strutted boldly toward the exit, my t-shirt and red v-neck sweater the only protection for my upper body. I made quick, long-strided leaps, hoping to be the first out the door. I looked back; all those fools were poking, taking their time. Yes! I was first! I rammed open the door and instantly the moist, warm steam-heated air was replaced by the frigid, wet sheets of atmosphere so prevalent on Coldest Day. My little weenie shriveled to the size of a baby carrot and I exclaimed, "Jesus, Mary, and Joseph!"

I was convinced that statement was not swearing, as it was such a common expression at our house. Marnie Rolls felt otherwise.

Marnie stood directly behind me and she threatened, "Sean Raven I'll tell Sister Boniface!" Only when she said it sounded like, "Shaw Rave ahl tel siss bohuface!" Marnie Rolls was hearing impaired, we called it deaf in those days, and she had a speech impediment. Most of us had learned to distinguish her words. She had two monster-size hook-around-the-ear hearing aids that connected via a wire to a 3x5 inch battery pack in a leather holster that was strapped to her chest in a halter-like fashion. Marnie was sharp as a tack and as irritating as stepping on one barefooted. When she was really pissed she would adjust the dials on her battery pack until they squealed like a redneck's tires on a Saturday night.

I had to get away from her and into the shelter of the bus. I sprinted to that yellow transport and prayed she would not sit next to me. The plastic seat cover on the bus crackled from the cold as I sat, and shortly my butt felt the sting of frozen rock-hard vinyl and sent a shudder up my spine. My prayer went unanswered. Marnie sat next to me and said, "You ha to si neh to Sissuh Bohuface." I turned my body toward the window and twisted my face toward her. I mouthed some nonsense words in her direction without making a sound. She knew this game well. She stood up and over me and pushed her puppy breath on my nose and her magnified eyes behind those oversized pink-plastic-framed glasses glared at mine and she screeched over and over again.

"Wha? I cat heah you!"

"Wha? I cat heah you""

"Wha? I cat heah yu!"

I was in Hell. I was in Hell. I could feel the gnashing of teeth the nuns had told us about so many times. "In Hell," they would drone, "There will be the gnashing of teeth and a great darkness." I had not known until that moment in the bus next to Marnie Rolls what the gnashing of teeth meant. I was grinding mine to a fine powder.

The bus had one working heat vent that dried and kept warm the driver's window and sometimes the driver, other than that, it was a giant, yellow Coleman

Cooler in the winter and a pizza oven in the summer. Of course the bus never warmed up, and Marnie never let up. To this day I wake up once or twice a year in a cold sweat re-living the bus ride from hell. She went on and on squawking in her impeded manner, her battery box screaming all the while. I could not move. The shivering cold, her foul breath, and the noise made mush of my brain. To top things off our regular bus driver called in sick so Father Nelson drove us, and he delighted in hitting every bump which made the shockless vehicle bounce every few hundred feet throwing me even closer to Marnie. "Let me out!" I once cried, but, ironically, it fell on deaf ears. Mercifully the bus finally stopped at my house.

I bolted from my seat and burst open the door, ran into my house and down the basement stairs. I nearly hugged the gray-black, ash-covered, coal-burning furnace. Within fifteen minutes I was warm, dry, and sucking soot from the old monstrous furnace. The fire from the monster put a glow inside of me. I also enjoyed the quiet burn of the coal inside.

Chapter Two

By 4:30 that frigid afternoon Mom was starting dinner, and since it was Tuesday, dinner was Chili. Monday was spaghetti, Tuesday chili, Wednesday beef and noodles, Thursday sausage and sauerkraut, Friday salmon patties, Saturday was leftover day and Sunday was fried chicken, my personal favorite. We had potatoes with every meal. We had potatoes mashed, hashed, slashed, sliced, diced, chipped, Frenched, boiled, baked, or covered with cheese, or margarine (butter was too expensive) and on rare occasions sour cream. We like our potatoes. We like our Irish heritage. In my twenties I married the first woman who treated me to a variety of meals. She was not Irish, she was not Catholic (that nearly got me thrown out of the family) but I will never forget her, and that is a story for another time.

We were having chili that night, hmmmmm . . . I began to form an idea on how to get moved away from Sister Boniface's desk. Everyone knew Sister Bony Face (the nickname came naturally considering her large beak and her dried apple-core complexion) had the most sensitive schnoz in Indiana. I mean, you could tell by looking at the sheer size of it, and she always smelled of pine cleaner which we were sure she used like a sailor uses Old Spice. The pine smell hid the odor of children, which she once told us smelled of wet dog and burnt trash. So, I figured if I ate a couple gallons of Mom's chili, which produced more gas than the Rock Island Refinery in Indianapolis, and had a midnight snack of hard-boiled eggs, popcorn, and leftover sauerkraut, then I could "stinker' my way away from Bony Face's desk. That night I ate with the unbridled passion of a wild mustang, I singled out the largest beans in the chili pot and swallowed them whole without chewing. I finished three bowls of chili. Later that night I raided the refrigerator and ate four hard-boiled eggs, which Mom had made for Wednesday's potato salad, I tried to eat some pickled pig's feet which my father considered a delicacy, but I just could not. I did swill down some very cold, very old sauerkraut.

The next morning my stomach was a roiling carbonated river of lethal gases. I was ready to stinkify the air around Bony Face's desk. It should have been no problem, as I was the master of silent but deadly farts—SBD's.

Marnie Rolls stuck her tongue out at me as I got on the bus for school. She was mad at me from the day before, and I at her. In fact I had yet to forgive her for telling Bony Face that I nicknamed her "Bony Face" but, I did not get in trouble over that because when Marnie told on me, it sounded something like this:

"Shaw Ravey cawe you Bowi Face."

"Yes, and." Sister patiently replied.

"Shaw Ravey cawe you Bowi Face."

"Yes, get on with it Marnie."

"Shaw Ravey cawe you Bowi Face!"

"Well, that is my name, now go sit down, Marnie, and do not raise your voice to me again."

Once in a blue moon things just work out for the best. Anyway, back to that morning. Marnie mercifully strode by me indolently, and she let me sit alone. I took this to be a sign from God that it would be a good day. Signs can be misleading. I made noises as I walked from the bus to the church (we went to mass every day before school) little mini farts escaped with each step. One noise was curiously absent though. I noticed the zip had left my old rust-colored corduroy coat. When it was new it would go zip zip zip whenever I moved my arms. Now it only went flp flp flp. The cords had worn off from me walking like a hyperactive goose stepper. It is a fourth-grade boy's job to make noises, especially bodily function noises, and I was quite proud of the little symphony my farts and corduroy flp's made on the walk to mass.

The mass started as it always did with the girls on one side of the church and the boys on the other side; we were well behaved in school, but we were angelic in church. Bony Face kept a long wooden pointer with her at all times, and if someone put their butt on the pew when they should have been kneeling, she would silently slither up behind them and poke them in the small of the back. I will tell you it straightened the miserable little wretch up in a hurry! I still have marks back there.

In the middle of mass the inner tummy rumblings began in earnest. I was kneeling and the first cramp imploded. I doubled up to stop the pain, which of course put my butt on the pew. I straightened up in anticipation of the pointer. I doubled up. I straightened up. I doubled up and straightened up again. I must have looked like the old dunking giraffe toy. Bony Face poked me just for good measure, at that point a quick crackling fart popped out. To my surprise Bony Face retreated. Of course Ricky Smart, the retarded boy in our class who was next to me began giggling which caused a chain reaction. Soon all the boys were laughing, and the more we tried to stifle the laughter, the louder we got, and when Ricky shot a snot rocket in his attempt to stop laughing our cacophony made Joshua's trumpets sound like Tinkerbell's greeting.

Then the unthinkable happened, Father Nelson with his bald, sweaty head glistening red with anger actually stopped the mass! **HE STOPPED THE MASS!** With his short fleshy finger he pointed at our group and sonic-boomed out in his big mass voice only one word, "**BOYS**" It sounded like God's thunder. We instantly shook with fear expecting God himself to pluck us from the pew and dash us on the stone floor of the altar in a bizarre Catholic sacrifice hitherto unknown. Thankfully, we were spared, and Father Nelson just shook his fat digit at us, turned around and continued mass in the ancient language of the church. Shortly we settled back into our normal ritual of mass, which included making Latin translations to suit us. So, O ra pro nobis became, Oh rotten oranges, and et cum sprit tu tu o became a can of spit on you to go, and so on. Well, we survived another mass, all of us quite aware that if we were suddenly killed by a runaway bus, we would go directly to heaven because we had just left mass, which means we were in a state of grace. There would be no prison time in Purgatory, no lingering in Limbo, just pass go, collect $200.00 and go straight to heaven. It truly was an ecstatic feeling.

I had extra gas-propelled locomotion behind me on our brief walk from the church to the classroom. Ricky Smart was directly behind me and had to suffer through the stench. Those brief moments fluctuating between church and school brought tremendous relief for me but undeserved agony for Ricky. Ah, the great Catholic dichotomies, good and evil, heaven and hell, Jesus and Satan, temptation and redemption, farts and roses.

Now, Our Lady of the Golden Flower Catholic School had more than its share of speech-impeded children. Ricky the Retard (as we coldly, not maliciously, called him in the pre-politically-correctedness days) not too much unlike Marnie Rolls', "You tink you tink, Yonni!" Ricky took quite a chance talking in line, which was strictly forbidden, as was talking in church, talking in class, talking in the lunch room, staring out the window, doodling, drawing, dancing, singing, looking up girls dresses, picking your nose, scratching your privates, sleeping, daydreaming, or any activity unrelated to classroom work. It seemed to the rest of us, however, that Ricky never got in trouble, no matter how much he talked or babbled during those specific quiet times. We figured old Bony Face and the rest of the nuns were afraid of Ricky because he was so tremendously strong. One day Ricky picked up Jim Beverage and threw him across the playground. Ricky was mad at Jim because Jim had mocked Ricky's speech; naturally few of us were sorry to see Jim Beverage crying. He had a way of annoying you even if he didn't pick on you personally. He was rich, which none of the rest of us were, and it is easy to dislike rich kids, especially rich obnoxious children who make every effort to point out how fat, or uncoordinated, or un-athletic, or how short you are, or how crooked your teeth were, or how your Mom always packed peanut butter and mayonnaise sandwiches for your lunch (Jesus, no wonder I was a fat kid). Am I running on about this too much? Anyway, Ricky did not get punished for that incident even though the school was rife with witnesses. At that point we were pretty sure the nuns did fear Ricky, and maybe, just maybe, they did not like Jim Beverage either (Camel through the eye of a needle, if you know what I mean). Maybe they pretended not to see it happen and no one reported it, that's for sure. So. Ricky talked, snorted, and giggled on the short walk between church and school. He would spend the remainder o the day reeking of fart and incense.

I took my dreaded seat next to Bony Face. I began the assault almost immediately, pffft-SBD, pffft-SBD, pffffffffeeeeeeeeet—squeaker SBD. One right after the other in rapid succession just like the staccato of a Bar gun used in the best TV show ever—Combat starring Vic Morrow whose untimely death will be cruelly remembered in a series of helicopter jokes.

Bony Face eventually raised her head and looked over her black, horn-rimmed glasses at me then returned to her lesson plan, or prayer book, or crossword puzzle, or whatever the hell she did at her desk.

I kept the attack up pfft, pfft, pfft, pfft, squirt. Oh no! The last one was wet. The cheeks of my butt were squishy! I now had to draw on Herculean strength! I had to hold it in! Oh my, it bisected me like a magician's assistant in the sawed-in-half trick. Those insidious internal farts began to rumble, explosions in my tummy rivaled the Battle of Britain. I squeezed my butt cheeks together with all the fanatic fervor of a Holy Roller at Springtime Revival.

Finally, Bony Face looked at me and said, "Sean go to the restroom."

"Thank you Sister," I said in the obligatory Catholic schoolboy response.

Negotiating my way to the restroom proved a challenge. I walked with my heels together and my buttocks in an iron grip, praying all the way. "Hail Mary" squirt, "full of grace" squirt, "the Lord is with thee" squirt. "Please Mother Mary; don't let me leave a shit trail to the restroom. Sorry about the words <u>shit trail,</u> Mother Mary." Squirt. I loudly finished my prayer when I got to the boy's room. I must have looked like a wounded one-legged duck with my arms flailing, and my feet joined together paddling along. Thank God no one saw me. I inched my pinched-butt way to the toilet, dropped my pants and let fly a shower of digested sauerkraut, chili, and hard-boiled eggs. I looked down and was shocked to see I had soiled my underpants completely, and there was spillage on my pants as well. I had to think. I knew I could not call my Mom to bring clean clothes. I could not buy new clothes. I could not break into the nunnery and steal a habit (nor would I wish to). The only thing left to do meant I had to wash the clothes in the restroom sink. I had to hold the rusty spring-loaded stainless steel faucet open with one hand while I washed the stains out with the other. That nasty pink liquid antiseptic-smelling soap that looked like Pepto Bismol (which I wished I had right then) did a fairly good job on my clothes. I managed to get my shirt wet while I was washing so I took it off for caution's sake. Soap, scrub, rinse, soap, scrub, rinse. I would have made quicker progress except I had to stop twice during this process to sit on the pot and relieve myself.

While I was on the pot the second time Jim Beverage came in. "Where are you, Sean?" He noticed the clothes in the sink. "Are you doing your laundry in here?" He laughed. He laughed hard. "Bony Face wants you back." He could not help but notice the smell and put two and two together. "You pooped your pants!" He laughed again on his way out.

"I did not poop my pants!" I yelled, but my reply was unheard as Jim could not have heard me above his own laughter. I knew he would tell everyone. My life was over. If I could have I would have flushed myself down the toilet along with my odoriferous wastewater. It could not possibly get any worse.

OF COURSE I WAS WRONG.

I jerked the sopping wet clothes from the sink and started wringing them in a spiral just like my Mom did right before she hung the clothes upon the line to dry. Then I flapped the pants wildly in the air in hopes of drying them more quickly. I saw myself in the mirror and I must admit it was a funny looking sight. I just wished my weenie was big enough to flop around more when I moved, like some of the older boys I had seen in the dressing room of the city pool. In later years we all had nicknames that reflected the characteristics of our weenies. There was Turtle, Tiny, Tank, Rocket Man, Elephant, Trigger, Corkscrew (I really felt sorry for that guy) and I was known as Shorty, damn it. Well, just as I had the garment above my head, the door flew open and Sister Boniface stood in its ancient oaken doorway.

OH MY GOD! A NUN SAW ME NAKED!
NO SWEET MOTHER MARY! SAY IT ISN'T SO!

The shocked look on her habit-ringed face would continue to flash back at me at the most inappropriate times (especially during sex) and without warning. Those flashbacks were a major contributor to the end of my first marriage, but that is a story for another time.

Bony Face made an about face and left me alone. I wrung out the underpants one more time, shook them, and put them on damp, just in case she decided to come back. I flailed my pants around in a frenzy, droplets of water spraying the smooth, cream-colored, ceramic tile that seemed to reflect humiliation off the walls.

While I was still flapping my pants around Paco Alvarez timidly poked his head around the entryway and said, "Sister Boniface told me to see if your were OK." "I'm fine." I lied. I had to make up something good. "The toilet blew up and got me all wet."

Paco looked at the toilet, which had no stall door in order to keep the horny Catholic boys from abusing themselves at school, and said "The toilet looks OK to me."

"Just the water blew up. It flushed up, just the water! I swear to God!" Oh shit, I lied and used the Lord's name in vain in one sentence. Oh well, three Hail Mary's penance and I would be back in good graces with God. That was the best thing about being Catholic; you could sin all you want, and as long as you went to confession you were all right. You just had to hope your death came right after confession (or mass) which is why they have the last rites, but we called it extreme unction in those days, a mysterious Latin name for a sacrament you just had to have on your death bed, or go straight to hell no matter what kind of life you lived.

Paco quietly stared at me then turned around. What a surprise! Paco seemed satisfied with my up-flushing story and went back to class. I pulled my still-wet pants on and followed shortly thereafter.

I hesitantly opened the door to a room full of astonished faces. Although fraternizing with our fellow students was strictly forbidden during class, an intricate system of communication including notes, whispers, sign language, and lip reading had been in full force. Paco, who sat in the back of the class, had started the confab, and by the time it reached the front of the room a convoluted story had it that I survived a dangerous assault in the boys' room by a known communist. It was considered a miracle that I was alive, but in 4th grade at Our Lady of the Golden Flower many things were considered a miracle. When Dennis Riley got the cast off of his broken arm a week early it was thought of as a divine intervention of quick healing, and thus a miracle. We later found out the cast itched so badly that Dennis used his grandpa's tin snips (Grandpa retired as a tool and die maker) to cut it off himself. His dad got angry, but reconsidered when Dennis reminded him that would save him the cost of another doctor's appointment. When Marnie Rolls thick glasses saved her fragile eyesight from an errant fly ball on the playground that was considered a miracle. So I was now the recipient of a miracle, this would definitely raise my status in the definite pecking order of popularity in room 4b.

Sister looked at my still-wet pants and red face (miracle or no miracle I was still embarrassed) and said, "Sean, you may move your desk to the back, next to Paco." Yes! My fart attack had worked! This was better than sitting next to Bony Face, but it was not the optimum seat for a miracle-boy trying to raise his stature with the other fourth graders as Paco Alvarez was at the bottom of the popularity list in room 4b at Our

Lady of the Golden Flower School. Paco had a constant sad look on his round Mexican/Indian face, which was surrounded by a soup-bowl haircut that preceded the Beatles coif by a couple years. His big brown eyes remained open most of the time and he did not blink nearly enough. He wore what appeared to be the same clothes every day, a white t-shirt and black dress pants. I am sure he would have worn blue jeans had they been in the dress code. At least we did not have to wear uniforms like they did at Cathedral Elementary.

Jim Beverage and the rest of the popular boys called him Paco Taco, or Tomato, or greaser. Now I had to sit next to him. Paco rarely had an expression on his face other than the sad look, but when I moved my desk next to him I think I saw a thin smile cross his face. He probably felt happy not to be the only loser in that lonely corner of the room. What a horrible day it had been, at least a surprise for me at home would cheer me up later.

As I said, Paco was at the bottom of the pecking order preceded by Ricky Smart, Marnie Rolls, and then me. Paco took up the rear because he was Mexican and poor, Ricky because he was retarded, Marnie for her impediments, and me because I was short, fat, and clumsy.

I was only marginally happier than before. I sat wet, embarrassed, and next to Paco Alvarez, my butt itched, and my stomach still exploded internally. The farts became less and less frequent as the day wore on but each time one slipped out Paco and I would get the giggles. As everyone knows, the more you try to suppress the giggles the harder it becomes to control them. One look from Sister Bony Face brought us back to Catholic-schoolboy good behavior each time, but each time also brought with it a little "Hershey squirt". That was one of the few times I saw Paco smile and heard him laugh. The rest of that school day crawled in the same miserable routine of every school day there. Prayer, spelling, prayer, lunch, prayer, geography, prayer, religion class, prayer, recess, prayer, art, prayer, music, lots of rote memorization for all, no physical education, finally prayer and dismissal.

At that time I put on my zippless, not zipper less, corduroy coat and walked in my now drier, but wrinkled and scratchy pants to the bus. I sat my sore butt on the cracked vinyl seat, Marnie sat next to me (I could not escape that cretin). She did one of those nose wrinkling contortions and threw her head back to get her glasses to slide back into place. She turned to me and said, "You poo yuh pants in school."

"Shut up Marnie," I screamed.

"You sai shu up ahl tell Sissuh."

"Go ahead and tell her I don't care. Just shut up, Marnie!"

"You poo yuh pants."

"You poo yuh pants."

"You poo yuh pants."

A blue knuckled rage overcame me. I stood up and over her and wrapped my hands around her neck. I could feel the hearing aid cords imbedding themselves in her windpipe. All sound to me ceased to exist in my rage, as if Marnie somehow transferred her deafness to me. I saw her complexion turn from rosy red to a startling shade of cyan. The terrified look on her face brought me back to my senses and I stopped myself before I killed her. She cringed and curled up tightly against the window. I turned my back to her and felt a rush of emotions including satisfaction, vindication, guilt, and oddly enough, titillation. The bus driver that day, Ricky Smart's dad, who also served as the school janitor belatedly shouted, "What's going on back there?!" No one answered him.

The other kids on the bus were looking at me incredulously in total silence. Jim Beverage had a silly grin on his face. The sight of Jim's face perked me up; I figured his estimation of me must have gone up a notch or two. Even though I hated Jim Beverage, I wanted him to accept me into the inner circle of the popular kids which included the most beautiful girl in the world, Peggy Myers.

Marnie remained silent the remainder of the bus trip. She recoiled violently every time I turned even slightly towards her. I tried to apologize several times, but words simply would not escape my lips. I never did apologize. Marnie, if you should happen to read this, sorry.

When I got up to leave, Jim Beverage smiled at me. I just knew he was going to commend me on a job well done for silencing Marine Rolls, but instead, he said, loud enough for most of the bus to hear, "You pooped your pants!" The laughter rang in my head as I ran off the bus with my reddened face pointed to the ground, and it rings to this day when gloomy moods hit me.

Chapter Three

The moment I walked through the front door my older sister Evvie, who attended the junior high school next door to our elementary school, which started and ended each day earlier than our school so our one bus could be put to the ultimate good use, greeted me at the door with a taunt, "It must be nice to be the favorite." She said bitterly.

My dismal mood nearly vanished at this statement. This could only mean one thing; Mom and Dad had bought me something. This was a rare occasion indeed. Could it be a new bicycle? No one in our family had ever had a new bike, except maybe my cousin Gary, whose father sold cars and they were rich, but certainly no one in my immediate family, which included my older sisters Betty and Sara, and my brother Ed, all of who had already moved out of the house and were "on their own". Evvie and I were pleasant surprises, as my mother used to tell us, that God gave her to keep her young. Maybe the gift was a BB gun, or a pair of fitted roller skates, not the kind you hooked to your own shoes, but the black-leather, honest-to-God roller skates. Hot anticipation rose in me like a fiery July sun.

I cautiously went to the kitchen where you could almost always find Mom. She was busy preparing Thanksgiving dinner, which was the next day and the only Thursday of the year we did not have meat loaf. Mom's customary 'Hi honey" was replaced with, "Are you looking for something Sean?"

"No" I lied once again that day. "I just wanted to see how you were doing."

I bounded my sore butt up the stairs to my room, flung open the door, fully expecting to see a new go-cart, or bicycle, or fire truck, or BB gun, instead lying on my bed was a new winter coat. You might think I was disappointed, but I most certainly was not. I had goose bumps! Anything new for us was as rare as an Amish corvette. It was a deep blue coat with white anchors on it like so many polka dots. The coat had a big silver zipper with a small metal anchor on the end instead of the normal tie-shaped tab. Best of all, it was a plastic coat with mysterious crunchy padding inside. I tried it on and waved my arms vigorously. Swish, swish, and swish it chanted, ah! A new sound to replace the fizzled zip of my old corduroy coat. I was anxious to try it out in extremely cold weather as I anticipated, and rightly so, that it would make loud crackling sounds in the bitter cold. I was extremely pleased with my new gift, and I knew what I would be thanking God and my parents for the following day on Thanksgiving. I knew my older siblings would complain that Evvie and I were spoiled, that they never had it as good as Evvie and I, but I did not care. I cherished that coat long after it left me.

Chapter Four

I was apprehensive about returning to school after Thanksgiving break. The morning had started off badly enough. First, we were out of toothpaste, so Mom made us brush our teeth with baking soda and rinse with hydrogen peroxide. That stuff tasted awful, and it felt like sand in your mouth, and it smelled like that infected cut I had on my finger the summer before when it oozed with that yellowish goo. I had a fleeting thought, "What if they actually made toothpaste with those ingredients someday?" Then I laughed to myself thinking, "What a ridiculous notion that is. Who would be stupid enough to buy something that awful?"

The breakfast was our normal toast and tap-water tea. Every morning Mom would make toast and put the nearly frozen margarine out for our use, and every morning I would shred the toast with the super hard margarine. The lukewarm tea was always as sweet as Pollyanna's personality.

"I wish they would make a soft margarine." I griped.

My father spoke up, finally looking away from his newspaper, "they will someday, but the Russians probably will do it first."

Evvie and I looked at each other with a knowing glance. Our father was obsessed, as was most of the nation at that time, with Russia and communists. We were expecting him to break into his spiel about how technologically advanced over the United States the Russians were since Sputnik. We braced ourselves for his speech, but then were quite relieved when he returned to his cigarette and newspaper.

I wore my new sailor coat, as I called it, with pride upon my return to school. It seemed the events of the previous week were overshadowed by the appearance of my new coat. Even Jim Beverage gave it an envious look. Of course the always hateful Marnie Rolls had her comment, "Yur coa Ih ugy!"

Paco Alvarez remained his quiet self, with his strong and sad dignity, seemingly unaffected by all of us who surrounded him. I swear Peggy Myers, the most beautiful girl in the world, actually smiled at me. Others verbalized their admiration. Dennis Riley said, "Nice coat, Sean." None of us in those days received new things often.

Sister Bony Face made two announcements that day, both of which were welcome news to me. The first concerned the upcoming Christmas season and our annual gift exchange. We would once again pick names from a hat, which was a green felt bowler left over from St. Patrick's Day, and then we would buy a small gift for whomever we picked. The drawing would take place after lunch, but then we needed to write our names on impossibly small pieces of paper given to us by Bony Face. Something was going on in the room which I quickly figured out; people were making their name-papers into shapes as a secret signal to their friends.

The second announcement was about next semester's Safety Patrol. Only the best behaved boys were in the running for Saftey Patrol (girls were considered too fragile for this dangerous job) so if you wished to be considered for a Safety Patrol position, you had to begin behaving now. That white one-shoulder harness with the bright silver badge was desired by almost all of the fourth grade boys. The power, the respect, oh my!! Three of us had to be trained for an entire semester to learn the intricacies of safe bus boarding, traffic control, and pedestrian cross walking, one of those three boys would be me! I could see the red, white, and blue certificate framed in our hallway now! SEAN RAVEN—CERTIFIED MEMBER OF THE SAFETY PATROL presented by Our Lady of the Golden Flower School. Our behavior between now and Christmas break would decide who would be the next three Safety Patrol Boys, I knew I would be absolutely saintly.

After lunch the fateful name drawing was held. All through lunch I prayed to God that I would draw Peggy Myers, the most beautiful girl in the world. I thought she might have liked me too, because that day she hit me in the arm in the lunch room, which is a pretty good sign that a girl likes you.

The Christmas/St. Patrick's Day hat had to be passed around twice, once to deposit our names and once to withdraw them. I carefully watched each student place their paper in the hat. Peggy Myers, the most beautiful girl in the world, who sat in the front row, was the first to place her name in. Her paper was triangular in shape. Since hers went in first I would have to reach in deep to retrieve it. Dennis Riley made a tiny airplane of his; Ricky Smart crumpled his into a ball. Some of the other kids cut corners on their paper; Marnie Rolls, who had many terrible habits including picking her nose and eating the boogers, had sucked on hers. Much to my dismay, Jim Beverage also made a triangle of his paper. He was the one person I did not want to get in the Christmas exchange, so if I got his triangle instead of Peggy's I would die. Wait a minute—they made the same shape? Surely Peggy Myers, the most beautiful girl in the world, did not like Jim Beverage. It had to be a coincidence, I was the last to drop my name in, and I would be the first to draw one out. Bony Face took the hat, covered the opening with a notepad, and shook the hell out of it. "Nooo!" I thought. I would have to rely on my sense of feel for the triangular shape.

Bony Face held the hat above my head and gave me the nod to reach in and pull out my selection. I rummaged around trying to feel the shape. I grabbed what I thought might be a triangle, but it was not; it was a simple square. I unfolded the paper and a faintly written barely visible, very small "Paco" could be found in the center, bisected by the crease of the fold.

I tried not to show my disappointment. I watched the room. Some faces were bland; others appeared the way I now felt, when they found out for whom they were to be Secret Santa. Jim Beverage pulled out a triangle and he beamed when he saw Peggy Myers, the most beautiful girl in the world, signature.

We were under strict orders not to reveal who we drew, so naturally by the end of the day everyone knew who their secret Santa was. Ricky Smart drew my name which did not disturb me because everyone knew his mother would pick out the gift, and she was a smart shopper, and she would spend the twenty-five cent limit wisely. The gift exchange would take place the day before the Christmas break.

Most of us were given the privilege of doing our own shopping for this small gift, so my sister Evvie and I walked downtown on the Saturday after the Annunciation. (Which was December 8th; the day the Angel told the Virgin Mary she was going to have God's child.) This was traditionally when the Catholic Christmas shopping season officially began. It began to start earlier each year until it became the year-round activity it is today.

We went to Kresge's Department Store, which later became K-Mart. We each had a quarter allotted to us for the gift exchange and an extra dime to share just in case. We only lived three blocks from the downtown in our small community, so we walked.

When we entered Kresge's we separated and went to our favorite departments, Evvie to costume jewelry and I to the toy department. I passed the pet area on the way and whistled and hummed simultaneously, which shut the parakeets up. I eyed the painted turtles, which were 24 cents, and many of them had really neat designs painted on them, but I feared Paco may not have an aquarium to keep one in, and most importantly the turtle would probably not survive until the Christmas exchange. The last turtle I bought crawled under the refrigerator, expired, and we forgot about it until we smelled something funny coming from underneath there.

The selection in the toy department was small in my price range, a bag of plastic soldiers, 19 cents, a bag of marbles, 25 cents, a bamboo whistle, 23 cents, and a tin cap gun. Then I spotted the best gift for Paco. It was a balsa wood airplane with a rubber band motor and rubber wheels on metal pins. It also had flaming decals to stick on its fuselage, and at 24 cents I could afford it. Perfect! I pulled the airplane off its display hook and then saw plain glider planes behind it. These were undecorated, unpainted gliders with no decals to attach, with no rubber wheels, but they were only ten cents each and I could buy two of them with a nickel left over for me. With the extra dime Mom gave us just in case we needed it, I could buy for the first time in my life the dime Coke instead of the nickel Coke at the oval shaped soda fountain and restaurant in the center of Kresge's, which is where we always ended our shopping excursions.

I could not finish the entire 16 ounces of cola and shared the remainder with Evvie. I could not imagine then 6 ½ ounce Coke bottles being replaced by such a large amount of drink as it is today. We lingered in Kresge's a while longer, we tried on reading glasses, attempted to get a free weigh-in at the penny scales (it stopped at 50 pounds until you put your penny in) but we had long since surpassed that weight. We always hoped it would give our weight anyway, just so we could say we got something for free, of course we could always weigh ourselves at home, but that would not be the same. We spent another half hour "window shopping" down each aisle longing for all the doo-dads and gizmos. I demonstrated to Evvie my whistle-hum which once again silenced the parakeets in a hurry; we laughed as they instantly quieted down and cocked their heads in a look of consternation. We tried on reading glasses and lied to each other about how great we looked in glasses. Somehow it made you want to wear glasses. Years later in high school I got my wish to wear glasses, and a girl even told me I looked like a fat Michael Caine in them, which was the best compliment I had ever received about my looks. I pretended to be the famous spy he played in the movies. We finally left the department store full with consumers' lust.

We took the alleyways home and dug through people's trash in search of discarded pop bottles. We rummaged around in old rusted and scorched oil barrels sifting through the ashes of burnt out trash for these glass bottles of gold; after all, they were worth two cents each even if they were blackened with soot. We also played a game with them. The bottom of the bottles had the name of the city in which they were manufactured and whoever got the most distant bottle won a valuable prize. The prize being the winner could smack the other's wrist with two wet fingers. We even had an arrangement with

Old Lady Simpson, one of our neighbors. We would return her empty cartons of pop and shop for her at the corner grocery store, in exchange for the bottle deposit. We would sign her sales receipt for her groceries and old man (anyone over twenty-five was old to us) Kinney would give us the cash for the bottles. It was an excellent arrangement, except that Old Lady Simpson barely consumed any food or drink, so our shopping treks only came once a month after her social security check arrived.

About a block from home my bladder started singing to me, soon it was wailing at me like Mario Lanza in an Italian costume musical.

"Evvie I gotta pee," I whined.

"We are almost home. You can hold it."

"I am holding it!" I screeched, and I was holding it. My hand was down my pants holding it with the authorized Dick the Bruiser Iron Claw Grip.

"OK, OK, go under the trestle.

The trestle was our favorite forbidden fortress. It was an ancient solid iron railroad bridge with enormous bolts holding it together. It formed a small tunnel over the street below. Mom forbade us to play on or near it, or on the railroad tracks as she always warned us if we got too close to a passing train the vacuum would drag us beneath its wheels and make ground hamburger of us. Mom was convinced we would fall off the trestle to our untimely death if we ever walked on it. So naturally it was with guilty pleasure that we almost played on the trestle and the tracks every day.

Evvie held my precious sailor coat as I climbed down the embankment and then up to the little space between the trestle and its concrete base. I laid on my side, and held onto the giant bolt at the base to keep my balance. I was afforded complete privacy, if not comfort, in this awkward position. I unzipped and began flooding the open space between the wall and me, but then the urine started moving back towards me. I couldn't stop the stream so I raised myself up on one hand and held the bottom of the trestle with my other, the pee river started flowing under my human bridge, just then a train whistle sounded and I was still peeing. Evvie shouted, "get out of there Sean!"

I was in a real pickle. I did not have a free hand to "shake the dew off my lily" as my dad used to say and I could not zip up or move without lowering myself onto the yellow river below me; the train was only yards away. I could see the headlines now **Boy Dies in Pee Puddle** or **Boy Pissed—Mom Pissed Off.** I only wanted to die with dignity. The engine roared on top of the trestle with the fury of a thousand lions. I screamed. The train was a long one carrying car after car of coal from southern Indiana on its way to Chicago. The engine and each car made a clump-clump sound as it rushed overhead on the trestle, and I felt the vibration of every one of them. I was delighted and surprised to find I was not crushed by the weight of the train as Mom had told me I would be if ever I was stupid enough to go under there. My arms were getting tired and the cold damp Indiana air was not evaporating the steamy mess below me, and it smelled bad. The train went on and on, my fingers were losing their sense of touch, and I knew I could not hold on much longer. I decided to throw myself sideways off the ledge with my feet and slide down the slanted concrete wall. I did so but scraped my exposed weenie on the concrete. I landed at the bottom of the embankment to a dreaded sight, my mother and a tearful Evvie in our green Plymouth station wagon, Mom had her Edgar Allen Poe face on (the one where she looked concerned, but at the same time she would happily abandon you in a pit with a razor sharp pendulum lowering towards you). I quickly spun around and replaced my tender weenie in my pants. I realized that twice this school year, three people, whom I did not wish to, had seen my little friend, my buddy, my pal Eli, my Johnson, Mr. Happy, Shorty. I was mortified.

Evidently Evvie thought my scream at the onset of the incident had been my death cry, and she raced home to get Mom. Mom had driven around the block and under the trestle in record time. Mom would not beat me like the lucky kid's parents whom I knew would, oh no, her punishment would be much worse. She would torture me with The Catholic Guilt Curse, an unwritten, but very much used part of the Catholic philosophy. She swung open the car door with one hand, while the other clutched a rosary. I knew she would wail and cry until I became a shaking, withering, blubbering jellyfish, totally void of any spine or skeleton. She pulled me to her chest and held me there with the strength of a spring-steel flying buttress. I could not tell who's beating heart I felt as we stood there, mine caused from guilt, or hers from panic. She cried and slobbered, occasionally waving traffic around with her right hand. She finally spoke in an old lady's voice, "Sean, you will be the death of me."

Mom drove us home at a snail's pace. When we got home Mom lit a candle and we had to say a rosary on our knees in thanks for my survival. I glared at Evvie for panicking, and she looked back at me with a hurt look on her face, obviously in preparation for when she too could put The Catholic Guilt Curse on her own children. It took two weeks for my penis to heal. I am still recovering from the embarrassment.

That Sunday, after I finished my homework, I decided to paint one of Paco's gliders. I took the long narrow tray of watercolor paints from Evvie's room. I could not decide whether to paint a cross, a star, or a target on the wings, so I opted for all three, a red star, a blue cross, and an orange target. I generously dipped the brush into the water glass and started with the red paint. I painted a star with boldness, but saw it was too watery as the balsa wood thirstily soaked it up. It looked like a pink marshmallow rather than a bright red star. I dipped the brush into the red paint again and tried to repair the damage, but it did not look any better. I decided to make it all red, like the Red Baron's plane. I dipped and brushed, dipped and brushed. It was hopeless. The wings began to curl from being waterlogged. It looked like a pink noodle airplane. I would have to give Paco only one of the gliders; I assumed he would not mind since it was just a quarter gift exchange at school.

Chapter Five

The last school day before Christmas break finally arrived. We had to do our normal work in the morning, and the time after lunch was reserved exclusively for our Christmas exchange party. Each of us was required to bring a treat, and everyone complied with that direction, of course I forgot to inform Mom until the night before and so I was forced to bring a bag of store-bought cookies, which I quickly and covertly laid on the dessert table. There were about 25 dozen cookies and one ½ gallon of eggnog on that cardboard table. The hallway water fountain got a workout that day. I devoured many cookies that day, including three Mexican Wedding Cakes, which we all assumed Paco Alvarez must have brought since he was the only Mexican in the room; however, it turned out they were brought by Marnie Rolls and they were left over from her sister's 16th birthday party from the week before, and boy they were really dry.

Soon after we started eating, Bony Face told us she had to go get the mail at the nunnery, and she would be right back. I actually believed she was going to pick up the mail, as it never occurred to me she might have really been using the rest room. None of us believed nuns could possibly have bodily functions. She put Marnie Rolls in charge and told us we may begin singing Christmas Carols. We sang Jingle Bells to start and soon heard singing from the other classrooms. We naturally came up with the idea of drowning out the other rooms with the volume of our voices. The fifth grade room responded in kind. It quickly degenerated into the Great Christmas Carol War of 1962. We shouted Silent Night. Angels not only heard us on high, but low, backwards, forwards, up, and down. We were screaming our joy to the world, and to anyone else who would listen. Of course, we knew Bony Face would eventually show up, and her stooge, Marnie Rolls, kept saying "Shu up! Shu up! Be quieh!"

It goes without saying we totally ignored Marnie. Even Paco Alvarez looked like he was having fun, but just as we were bellowing Away in a Manger Bony Face burst into the room waving her wooden pointer over her head like Moses did with this staff when angered at the idolaters. The pointer came slamming down on the cardboard table and a volcanic shower of cookie crumbs erupted into the air. We froze in mid song much like we did when playing the statue game. None of us moved. Only Marnie Rolls smiled.

Bony Face yelled **"TAKE-YOUR-SEATS"** punctuating each word with a pound of her pointer. The other classrooms became quiet too. Her body was shaking from anger and she walked slowly with the pointer in her left hand, and with her right she seemed to be massaging her left arm in order to give it more strength to hit with. Her demeanor dared us to try anything, anything at all. Of course none of us did. Her breathing slowed and she said, "Lay your heads down on your desks." We did, as this was the universal way to calm a classroom down at our school. When a leader suppresses a class day after day, it is amazing how quickly they revolt or turn wild when unsupervised. It is also amazing how quickly they return to their servile selves when the authority figure returns. That was us.

We had to keep our heads down on the desk and remain completely quiet for 20 minutes, an incredible amount of time for fourth-grade Christmas partiers. Ricky Smart fell asleep, his arm dangled to one side. Slobber began to form at the corner of his mouth and drooled in a long stream parallel to his arm. I could see that several of us with this view were watching the spit waterfall with fascination. It seemed hot in the room, too much excitement, my mother would say.

After the punishment time was up Sister Bony Face said, "Class, you may get up. It is time for the gift exchange. I will pass out the gifts." She unlocked the closet behind her desk where she had us deposit the gifts. She pulled them out one at a time and gave them to the recipient. She came to Paco's glider and said, "There is no name tag on this gift, to whom does it belong?"

I raised my hand and squeaked "That's Pacos'!"

"Well I guess Paco will know who his Secret Santa is, won't he?" She scowled at me. Like everyone doesn't know who his Secret Santa is I thought. I also thought "I wish old Bony Face would just die!" Paco took the gift and whispered "Thank you" to me.

My gift from Ricky was an orange yo-yo with no markings on it. I never could get the darned thing to work well. Jim Beverage beamed at Peggy Meyers, the most beautiful girl in the world, when he received her gift and she smiled back at him. Darn I hate when she smiles at him.

Marnie Rolls got Ricky Smart a small square metal loom with fabric loops to make potholders. Ricky just looked at it dumbfounded. Marnie showed him how to loop the pieces across the loom and interweave the other side with amazing speed and accuracy. I imagine Marnie Rolls' house was filled with potholders of every color possible. Eventually, Ricky just took the loops and flipped them off the end of his finger like a rubber band.

Paco opened his gift from me, slid the wing through the slot of the glider and smiled. He did a small test flight to my desk. When I caught it he smiled and said "Thanks Sean." We all went home and wished it would snow. It never seemed to snow in Indiana at Christmas time, and I later discovered statistically only once in every seven years does it do so. The beloved Christmas break started, and to our amazement Bony Face did not give us homework, two weeks of freedom, Christmas and New Years—what a relief, what joy, what excitement.

Chapter Six

On Christmas Eve morning Dad woke Evvie and I up early, which was quite unusual since we slept in every chance we could, and Mom preferred it that way since she said she could get so much more done with us out of the way. He roused us from bed and said in his loudest bass voice, "Come on, we're going to the country." The country was only about one mile from our house in our small town, and I tried to remind our father of that so I could sleep more, but he just laughed and smacked my behind to wake me again.

We got in the station wagon with Dad and we sleepily eyed the frost all around us. We both wondered where we were going. He scraped a hole in the frost of the windshield barely big enough to see out of and slowly started down the street. He hunched down to look between the steering wheel where the scraped area was, so he could see out onto the street. The defroster was blowing full blast and in a few minutes visibility was good. We did not travel far, maybe two miles.

Dad pulled onto a very long winding gravel driveway. Near the beginning of the driveway were a group of chicken coops followed by what looked to be a dozen or so playhouses similar to the one Jim Beverage had in his backyard. There was a light emanating from the playhouse closest to the main house. A thick electrical cord ran from the porch of the farmer's home to the playhouse in order to supply the electricity. Fifty feet from the playhouse stood an outhouse. We parked next to the main house and got out of the car. The back door opened and a rotund, hairy man stepped onto the cement steps. I wondered why he wasn't shivering as he was barefooted, wearing only bib overalls. He was shirtless and had very dark hair all over his arms. He smiled at my dad with his one eyetooth missing and he said, "Hello Brother Knight." (The official greeting of the Knights of Columbus) My father replied, "Hello Brother Knight."

"So these are your two hooligans," he observed. "You got a pretty girl there C.E., and the boy is not too ugly either, I've seen uglier." He tousled my hair at that point, and at that moment I swore to myself I would never do that to a child for as long as I live. So far, I have not done so. I know now he was trying to be funny, but children are so easily demeaned. "Come in for some coffee while I get my shoes on" There is something unusual about farmers, which is probably caused, or at least exacerbated, by their isolation. That is, many of them could care less what others think about their personal appearance, or the appearance of their dwellings or lawns. Many make huge signs to make political statements, or have great amounts of trash or broken machinery laying out for all to see. Some places look trashy, and the more remote the farm, the more unusual the displays. I once saw a sculpture of two pigs mating on the back of a rusted out flatbed truck. Not all farmers are like this at all, but Mr. Bob Daly certainly was. His kitchen should have been labeled a toxic wasteland. Dirty dishes were stacked two feet above the rim of the sink: dried mud was on the floor; magazines, newspapers, and letters were strewn about the kitchen table, and everything smelled of vinegar.

Bob Daly was a widower with grown children who had left the nest. His farm was large, and he was rumored to be one of the richest men in the county, which explained why some women paid him extra attention after church on Sundays. When I was much older my dad told me size did matter to women, but it was the size of your wallet that mattered most. I wondered how could Mr. Daly live like that, and I also wondered why we were there.

Bob Daly came back into the kitchen wearing a pair of dried-mud-covered boots. The shoestrings were so caked with mud I don't believe they could have possibly been tied, oddly enough the mud did not drop off as he walked. He handed my dad a cup of coffee (which he only pretended to drink) and asked "Do you want to take that with you?"

"Sure", Dad replied.

He waved us on and we all followed Bob Daly outside. I got a close up look at the electric wire leading from Bob Daly's porch to the first playhouse. I asked him about that. "Do you have electricity in your playhouses?"

"Playhouses? Oh, you mean those!" He pointed as he spoke. "That's where the tomato pickers live at harvest time. I keep one here all year to help out." Then he added, "He's a good man."

"He lives there?" I was stunned.

"Yep, and his wife and boy." He answered.

We walked a short distance to his big, paint-chipped, white airy barn. Bob Daly pushed the giant weathered door on its track to open it. The barn smelled musty and wet. There were many broken boards in the walls where rain could settle in and make a moist home for mosquitoes and gnats and all sorts of ugly critters come summer. There were old machine parts, conveyers, and a tractor, each in its own stall. Straw was strewn about the floor. At one point this barn held livestock, but now the only living creatures larger than a spider or a mouse were a fat momma English Bulldog and her one nursing beige puppy.

Bob Daly barked out, "She could have been weaned earlier, but I couldn't find anyone to take the little runt bitch." Evvie and I exchanged glances at this "bitch" remark and quietly giggled. We loved it when adults cussed. One of Bob Daly's massive hairy hands pulled the puppy away from its mother and put it in my arms. "Merry Christmas kids," He said.

My Dad smiled at me and then my sister put her arms out in a gesture indicating she wanted to hold the puppy. I obliged her wish, and when I turned around to face my Dad and thank him I saw something move outside the door. It was a quick blur of a shadow, maybe a goat, or a small deer, or a child perhaps. Maybe it was the tomato picker's kid. As we walked to the car I saw peripherally the mysterious object dart from behind the barn. It was another blur, but a child, undoubtedly, possibly dressed in a white t-shirt and blue jeans with rolled-up cuffs.

As we drove home I asked my father some questions.

"Why did Mr. Daly call the puppy the B word?"

He laughed, and then explained, "A female dog is called a bitch. That is why it's bad when you call someone a son of a bitch, because you are saying his mother is a female dog."

I was a little disappointed in his answer because I had always thought bitch surely had a much dirtier definition.

Dad looked at us sternly through the rearview mirror and said, "Don't think for a minute that I'm going to let you use that word every time you talk about that puppy. Speaking of calling her a name, you two need to name her."

The puppy was curled up in Evvie's lap shaking from the cold, or fear. I put my fingers to the pup's face and she licked them tentatively, staring at me with big brown eyes in a scrunched-up face. I thought she looked like Winston Churchill, but we couldn't call her Winnie since she looked like Winston Churchill, but Evvie thought that name should only be for Winnie the Pooh. Well, our great Aunt Martha looked a lot like Winston Churchill too, so I said, "How about Martha?" Evvie looked at me and we both started laughing. She had made the connection, and so Martha was named.

I continued to question my father, "How can those tomato pickers live in those tiny houses?" Dad put on the same expression he wore when he talked about the old days during the great depression when he was growing up. "People will do almost anything to survive. Things in Mexico aren't as good as they are up here, and the migrant workers, not the tomato pickers, are willing to suffer things in order to make their lives better."

I braced myself for him to continue by telling one of his interminable depression stories by putting myself into a trance. I learned this technique at a very early age and still use it to this day when my boss, or my wife, starts one of their tirades. My trance, however, was not necessary as Dad mysteriously became quiet.

We celebrated Christmas the next day with our usual gusto. My older siblings came into town and stayed for the day. They were happy to see us, but they had their own lives to lead in far-away places. We all received nice presents, including Martha, who got a black leather collar with a blank ID tag, which I would later inscribe with her name. Martha was supposed to be a family present, but the bond we shared through the years made her mine. She even slept in my bed, for which I was grateful because then I had something to blame for my occasional wet bed. Christmas night I went to sleep by thinking only 364 days until the next Christmas.

Chapter Seven

Bony Face assigned us a theme on our first day back from Christmas break. She told us to write about our favorite Christmas gift. I had no trouble choosing my beloved Martha as my favorite gift. I worked feverishly in the 30 minutes or so to complete the story. I told how she slept with me, I, of course left out the bedwetting part, and how she would lick or chew everything in sight. I did not tell how my great Aunt Martha looked like an English bulldog, but I said we named her after our ancestor because we loved her. Nuns love it when you sound all innocent, sincere, and loving in your themes, and if you can show somewhere in the paragraphs that you love Jesus too, then you could pretty much count on an A. I considered lying about getting a new rosary for Christmas, but opted for the truth and a lower grade. I later learned six people wrote about getting a rosary for Christmas.

Sister Bony Face startled us with a loud, "Time's up!" All of us jerked our heads up sharply in unison to look at her, all of us except Paco that is. He had his head down on his folded arms in front of him on his desk. Bony Face shot over to Paco's desk and when she stood over him we collectively held our breath in anticipation of her insane tirade. "Paco!" she bellowed. Her eyes were hot cinders, "where is your written work? Why didn't you write about your favorite Christmas present?" She slammed her wooden pointer on Paco's desk, which made us all jump up, including Paco, but then he lowered his head again. Bony Face fumed, "Answer my question Paco Alvarez!" He slowly raised his head again and lowered it again. Rage bolted from her eyes as quickly and fiercely as Torquemada's verdicts. Her pointer slammed on his desktop just millimeters from his from his fingers. "You answer me right now!" she shrieked as she shook. Paco shot his tear-stained face up and covered his eyes with his fingers, and she slapped his wrist with her oaken weapon. A teardrop splattered and rolled down his round cheek. "Uncover your face and answer me now!" she almost whispered this time.

"I didn't write," he squeaked, "because I didn't get anything for Christmas." Then he began to sob and laid his head down again.

"That is not true you little liar!" None of us could understand shy Sister Boniface was being so cruel; in fact, I still don't understand. Many of us began to weep very quietly so as not to suffer Sister's wrath. Marnie Rolls cried openly though, and she let the tears roll down her face without wiping them off; normally that would have revolted me because of the dirt track it left on her peach-fuzzy face, but for that moment it did not matter. Peggy Meyers had her face hidden behind her hands, but still manages to be the most beautiful girl in the world. Even the normally caustic Jim Beverage had that teary-eyed look.

Sister poked Paco in the small of his back and said, "You most certainly got something for Christmas. You received a gift in our classroom exchange." Paco raised his head again and displayed a blank face. All I could think about was, why had I been so selfish and cheap with that balsa airplane. 'Oh God make time go back' I silently prayed, of course time marched on. Then I silently prayed, 'Make Sister Boniface die!' I chanted it over and over again. 'Make Sister die! Make Sister die!'

Somehow I thought the wish would be more powerful if I kept repeating it, and I did, (to myself) 'Make Sister die!' Make Sister die!' I know others in the class felt the same way.

She made Paco take his desk out into the hallway to write his story while we continued with our class work. We turned in our papers and read silently from our history book. You could hear an occasional whimper from different points of the room. When he finished Paco had to knock on the door to get back in the classroom as Sister had locked the door. She scrutinized his essay over the top of her glasses, and then nodded towards him. "This will do," she said. She rubbed the top of his head but he shrank back in revulsion as she did. She pulled her left arm across her chest and massaged it as she said. "Bring your desk back in."

Only the sainted beauty, Peggy Meyers, the most beautiful girl in the world, looked at Paco immediately with a sympathetic gaze. It took the rest of us some minutes before we could gather the courage or composure to give him a wink or wave of the hand. All of us felt sympathy, shame, and fear: sympathy for Paco, shame for Sister Boniface, and fear for ourselves. None that I knew told his or her parents about the incident.

That was the way of the world them. Children did no complain about adults, especially the religious adult, to adults. We all feared the retribution Bony Face would surely have thrown our way if that incident became public knowledge.

Chapter Eight

The dull, gray learning-filled days of January and February crept along at the molasses pace of, well January. The sheer dullness of those months helped relieve the meanness of the incident, and a "miracle" that happened in February diverted our thoughts from it.

Now, in the days before, and during Vatican II (The great reformation of the Roman Catholic Church) there were thousands of saints, many of whom have since been demoted, including the once popular dashboard saint, Christopher. He was the patron saint of travel. There were, and are, patron saints of every conceivable condition, occupation, city, state, and disease. There are patron saints of carpenters, travelers, photographers, bricklayers, sailors, artists, lepers, lechers, Dubuque,

Iowa, Dublin, Ireland, Danville, Illinois, and those stricken with consumption, vapors, cancer, tuberculosis, and my personal favorite-sore throats. The patron saint of sore throats is St. Blaise, or as we thought of him, St. Blaze (sounds the same, but spelled differently.)

Catholic children knew February as the month of fire and ash. Most are familiar with the ash part, as Ash Wednesday normally came in February, but on different dates. This is known as a moveable feast. Catholics would be blessed with a scattering of ashes on their foreheads made in the sign of the cross by the priest. Ash Wednesday moved around because Easter changed every year. Its date had something to do with the full moon, and whether the Pope saw his shadow from the balcony of the Vatican on Christmas Eve, or something like that. The fire part was from St. Blaise Day. St. Blaise day was not a moveable feast and came on February third every year.

In 1963 St. Blaise Day was on a Sunday, and we mistakenly assumed we would be spared this ritual for that year-we were wrong-at the beginning of Mass on that Monday we were told we would have our throats blessed in honor of St. Blaise Day, since only the children of the parish had their throats blessed and the ritual was ignored for the adults on Sunday. Upon hearing this news the girls' side of the church quietly erupted in a frenzy of activity. The girls were looking for rubber bands, strings, or ribbons, anything that would work to tie your hair in a ponytail. The beautiful Peggy Meyers, the most beautiful girl in the world, was not as lucky as the rest of the girls, her hair was a flip and she found nothing to tie it back. The reason they were concerned is in order to have your throat blessed you had to kneel at the altar railing and Father Nelson would take two lighted white taper candles and make an x of them in his left hand, with his right hand he would make a sign of the cross and bless you with some Latin mumbo-jumbo, at the same time he would take his left hand and put the middle of the criss-crossed lighted candles and put it on your throat! This was scary as hell, especially if you were one of the last to be blessed because the candles have melted down to the point where they almost touched your ears. It was especially scary for beautiful girls with flip hairdos.

We dutifully lined up and knelt on our respective sides of the altar, boys on the right, and girls on the left. It went fairly well at first, with one or two exceptions when a boy would feel a nip of flame on his ear and squeak out a small protest. I noticed the boys who got burned were always troublemakers and had had run-ins with Father Nelson earlier. Vince Agneleri, a fifth grader and something of a black sheep in his family, seemed to get burned every year. It happened at the end of the blessing. Peggy Meyers, the most beautiful girl in the world, cautiously knelt down on the altar. She was the last student to be blessed because she kept letting people go ahead of her since she felt such fear and dread of those lit candles. We could see Father Nelson was getting tired and his hands were shaking as he started to bless Peggy. Peggy's eyes were as wide open as Christ's tomb as she watched Father Nelson shakily move those shortened candles towards her. Peggy's Mother must have put a lot of hair spray in Peggy's new flip hairdo because it caught on fire really fast. Peggy was quick to react since she anticipated the whole fiasco. She sprinted to the back of the church, dunked her head in the metal tray imbedded in the marble stand which held the Holy Water and came up wet, smelly, and except for one side of her flip do being gone none the worse for wear.

I heard muttering and whispers, "She used Holy Water to put out the fire!" (Holy Water was used strictly for blessings and to ward off vampires only. It was not to be used for any other purposes we were told repeatedly and emphatically.) "The Bishop will give her a special dispensation for using the Holy Water, surely." Special dispensations were cool. If you petitioned the Bishop to eat candy during school because you had low blood sugar he would give you a special dispensation to do it. Special dispensations meant 'It is ok to break the rules this time.' Then I heard Sister Maria Goretti say, "It is a miracle she was so cool headed about the situation." That was all it took to declare another miracle. The adorable Peggy Meyers, the most beautiful girl in the world, and I had something in common. We were both recipients of grammar school miracles, although hers had more validity than mine.

Peggy's Mom came to take her home, and it was a lucky thing she was a beautician and a wiz with hairstyles. All the popular girls went to her the week before Easter and had their hair done by her in her home beauty shop. Peggy, the most beautiful girl in the world, came back to school after lunch with a Pixie haircut. We were all stunned, but Peggy Meyers, the most beautiful girl in the world, managed to look even more beautiful than she had before. She looked like Audrey Hepburn, even prettier, if that is possible.

That night I had a dream. Peggy Meyers, the most beautiful girl in the world, was trapped in a two story wooden building, which was on fire. She was on the second floor and the staircase was burning. I raced up the stairs and scooped her in my arms and carried her down the burning staircase. Of course her hair was on fire, but I patted it out with my hands. She was completely bald. She looked ashamed of her lost looks, but I reassured her saying, "I will love you even if you turn ugly. It does not matter to me I love you." She then kissed me in my dream for the longest time.

I awoke with a protrusion in my underwear. The thing stood straight out and would not go down to its regular size. I felt all warm and tingly. I remembered something I overheard Father Nelson say to Vince Agnelneri on the playground during recess one day. "When the flag is a full staff you need to think of something else, like sports, or cars. Now go in the bathroom and throw some water on your face." I knew at that point Father Nelson was not talking about a real flag, and now I seem to remember that Father Nelson seemed to come out of the bathroom a lot with cold water on his face. So I tried to think of sports, but all I could imagine were the cheerleaders jumping up and down. Then I thought about cars, and car commercials on the television, and the beautiful models in the cars in the commercials, and they always seemed to be wearing these really low cut tops, and the camera angle looked down into the convertibles over the cleavage and onto the dashboard. That was not working. It still was stiff. So I went to the bathroom and threw water on my face. That did not help either. I tried smacking it, but I kind of liked that. I hung a cold washcloth on it. That did not help. Then I heard my father stirring and his bedroom door creaking. I felt waves of fear that he might see this phenomenon, so I locked the door. The fear made it go back to its original size, and I thought 'so that's how you get it to go down. There must be a better way, though.' Thank God there is a better, much more delightful way.

Many years after the St. Blaise day miracle, I learned from other Catholics who lived in other towns and cities that their priests never ever lit the candles on St. Blaise day. Father Nelson was unique and something of a rogue priest with a twisted sense of humor. He even had a one-day sex education class for us later in the year.

Chapter Nine

That year was the most event-filled of my time in elementary school. One morning our day started normally enough with prayer and schoolwork. We sleepily did our worksheets for nearly half an hour when someone looked up and saw something hanging above and behind Sister Bony Face's head. It hung from a metal track once meant for additional lighting. It looked like a blackened cob of corn suspended there. Through telepathy, or sonar, or some other signal we all soon found ourselves staring at it. Marnie Rolls first recognized it, and in her own way informed the rest of us, "O gah! A ba! A ba! A baaaaaa!" she screamed.

It was, of course, a bat, which we assumed, came literally from the belfry of the church to rest in our little classroom. Naturally panic ensued. The girls covered their hair, or hid beneath their desks. The boys tried to look brave and laugh it off, but fear plainly showed in most of our faces.

Surprisingly Sister Bony Face panicked as well. She started by raising her head toward the ceiling then toward the bat. She shrieked and shivered, then pulled at her headdress throwing her hands back and forth. She managed to tear the headdress off her head to reveal a most horrific sight. We saw a nun's hair! It was brown, short-cropped and messy. She kept rubbing her head with her hands. "Get it off! Get it off!" she wailed.

The terror caused by this immobile creature was absent from one among us. Paco Alvarez calmly rose from his seat, walked to the front of the room, pushed Sister's desk under the bat, climbed atop it, pulled a pair of pumpkin-colored work gloves from his back pocket and gently removed the bat from his perch. We sat open-mouthed in awe of his accomplishment. He then walked to the back of the room, opened a window with one hand and threw the bat out. It dropped to the ground. Paco was flooded with attention that day, and he spoke more than any other time I could recall, although, he mostly only said "Thank you" or, "it was nothing." I caught him smiling more than once and I, along with many others patted him on the back.

While our attention focused on Paco's courageous feat, Sister Bony Face had composed herself and once again appeared nun-like. She suggested that we pray immediately for she was sure this had been the work of the devil. She even said so, "That bat, that Lord of the Flies, was a sign, an omen, or Beelzebub himself! There is evil in this room!" She glared directly at me when she spoke the word evil, and she held that stare for several seconds. Well shit, somehow it was my fault that a bat had made a home in our room. Why me?

We prayed long and hard that day. Of course the news of the bat spread fast and wide like Jezebel's legs. It was the talk of the parish. At the end of the day Vince Agnelneri, a fifth grader tough guy who I admired more than anyone, approached me and asked how I liked the gift he hung in our room. As he spoke, he made the universal signal for silence on the subject by closing that invisible zipper across his lips. "How?" I asked.

"Come by tonight and I will show you," Vince replied.

Convincing my parents to drive me to Vince's house that night was easier than I had anticipated. My sister Evvie was going to a sleepover at her friend Carol's house, and oddly enough, my parents, who normally bickered quite a bit, were especially friendly towards each other. I even saw my dad give my mom a peck on the cheek, which made me gag. Dad even seemed anxious for me to go. "Sure Sean," he said with keys in hand, "Are you ready?"

"Well not quite. I have to get some books from my room," I lied. Vince told me to bring an extra pair of socks for some reason.

"O.K., no hurry, whenever." Dad seemed to say nervously.

Vince lived almost two miles from us on an Italian block, near the factory district. It only took about two minutes for us to get there. Dad hit the brakes a little too hard, and I had to catch myself by grabbing the dashboard as this was before seat belts, and long before seat belt laws. I gave Dad a disapproving look, and he curtly apologized, and then said, "I'll pick you up at nine o'clock." He reached across me and opened my door, which was quite unusual. "Jesus, Dad, what's your hurry?" I said to the bumper and a pair of fins as he sped away.

Vince's house looked like all the houses on the block, white one-story bungalows with small porches in front and an alley behind. A small statue of St. Jude stood on the grass beneath Vince's bedroom window, and Vince's eyes peered through two burn-holes in the screen of the window. "Hey Sean," he called, "come on in." 'Hey' had replaced 'hi' in those days, and in later years we only referred to each other by our last names. Language changes through the years, another example-we called cigarettes fags. Saying you were going to go suck on a fag has a much different meaning today.

When I entered his house, waves of odors washed over me, a mixture of garlic, beer, and soiled diapers; I couldn't help but hold my nose. I made my way to his room and I was able to avoid stepping on his little brothers and sister. He sat on the bottom bunk in front of his window. He brother Salvatore read a comic book on the top bunk. An old wooden crib was adjacent to the bunks where Al slept. Vince lovingly held in his hands what looked like a single barrel shotgun, but was actually a pump-powered air rifle BB gun. The more you pumped the lever on the barrel, the more power you gave the projectile. It was a beauty, and Vince caressed it like a first love. He grinned when he saw the awestruck look on m face, and said, "Do you like it?"

"Hell yes! Can I shoot it?"

"We'll see. Do you think you could hit a moving bat?"

"Yeah, I'm a good shot." I lied for at least the second time that day.

"Really?" He knew I was lying. "What kind of rifle do you have?"

Thankfully, before I could lie again, as I had no BB gun, his mother calleded to him, "Vince, Take care of the trash."

"O.K. Mama" he sang back. "You are going to love this, Sean." He slowly said each word, and then, "Grab that lighter fluid and matches off my dresser." I picked up the extra large can of Red Devil lighter fluid and the box of Ohio Blue Tip Matches, which didn't make sense because the tips were actually white. Vince carried his rifle and I followed.

The alley behind the Agnelneri's house had patches of gravel between thick new moan weeds. The alley dead-ended just west of their detached garage with a communal three sided cinder-block fire pit. A coal shovel leaned against the side of the pit next to a row of rusted 55-gallon oil drums. The neighbors would separate non-flammables, put those in the barrels, then burn their trash, scoop the ashes, put the ashes in the barrels, and once a week move the barrels out to be picked up by the trash collectors. This was the way most citizens of our community helped to reduce the waste in our city's landfill, only we called it the sludge pit, which laid only two blocks from downtown, and regularly filled with water and made an odiferous, primordial soup with every rainstorm. Unfortunately it was only one hundred yards from the creek, and the overflow ran off into it while the rest of the water quickly leeched into the tributary. Thankfully they filled it in and closed it down in a later, more enlightened era. The area is now a memorial to the sons we lost in Viet Nam.

Vince's Mom had the empty jars, bottles and other non-burnable materials already separated in a brown A & P grocery sack. I put that sack in their barrel and quickly scanned the other barrels for any treasures. I saw the burnt, blackened neck of a returnable Coke bottle

73

sticking out of the ashes of one barrel, but my hopes of the two-cent refund were quickly dashed when I pulled it out to find it was only the neck of the bottle.

While I was treasure-hunting Vince had piled the remaining trash at the back of the fire pit. He squeezed the lighter fluid can until it dented but there was very little of it left. He threw the empty can into his barrel and said, "I'll be right back." He sprinted to the garage and returned with a metal gasoline can, poured about a quart of gas on the trash, then returned the can to the garage. He came back, picked up his gun and pumped the lever with Herculean effort. He showed me how to place the match in the barrel with the bulbous tip creating a seal at the end. He explained how the match would flare when it hit the back cinder blocks and catch the trash on fire. He aimed, pulled the trigger and the match shot out . . .

Now, I have actually seen a crazed biker unscrew his motorcycle's gas cap and put his cigarette out in a full tank of gas with no adverse consequences. You see, the gas in liquid form is not nearly as explosive as the fumes, and Vince had spend so much time returning the gas can and pumping the BB gun there had been more than enough time for the gas vapors to permeate the area and create that intoxicating aroma.

When the match hit, it caused a thunderous explosion, and sent a fireball in the sky reminiscent of the mushroom clouds we had seen so many times on T.V. The force of the explosion knocked out three of the cinder blocks at the back of the fire pit, and blew soot out in all directions covering us from head to foot. Of course the sight of Vince's Mom waddle-sprinting towards us caused Vince's eyes to look like brown-yoked eggs in an iron skillet. She was waving a wooden spoon in the air and screaming in Italian, then in English she said, while smacking Vince with the spoon, "Vinnie, you bad boy, bad, bad boy! You must fix this before your gather gets home!" She scolded him for some time and finally returned to the house. By then, a crowd developed including Vince's siblings.

Vince and I worked quickly to replace the fallen cinder blocks, and then he got the hose out and washed down the fire pit. We washed ourselves as best we could with the frigid hose water. As I was bent over rinsing my hair something stung me in the butt. "Hey", I yelled, knowing it was too early for bees. "Did you shoot me, Vince?"

"No," he replied. "They did, **Publickers**!" He picked up his rifle and we scrambled to relative safety behind the fire pit.

"What are publickers?" I asked.

"You know, **publickers** the kids who go to George Washington."

"Why do they call them publickers?" I asked stupidly.

"Public school—pub lickers." He really emphasized the pub lick syllables of those words. "And they call us cat lickers!" he replied.

"Because we like cats?"

"No dumb ass, because we're catholic. Catholic—cat—get it?"

"Oh Yeah." I hoped Vince didn't think I was a complete idiot."

The Protestants darted behind the neighbor's garage. "Sean, those bastard's guns are CO2 powered. When their canisters are empty, they are helpless. You have to go out there and create a target 'till they are out of gas."

"What the hell, why me?"

"Because I have the gun."

I couldn't argue with that logic. Everyone knows the boy with the toy, or the ball, or the gun, holds all the power. So I ran back and forth in front of the fire pit getting stung and pelted repeatedly. I covered my face as best I could. It didn't hurt too much when they nicked my thick jeans, or sweatshirt, but the occasional BB that struck my hands or head really bit. After only a short time I could feel the trajectories losing power. That is when I ducked back behind the fire pit with Vince. He had that BB gun cocked to hyperspace. He stood up, aimed at the fleeing publickers and hit one in the elbow. "I winged him!" he exalted. He furiously cocked the lever again and got off another shot at the three running dungarees and sweats, hitting one in the butt. "And stay outa here!" he yelled after them. Victory was ours. We felt exuberant as Caesar at Pompey.

It took a few minutes for us to come off of that high and get back to work cleaning our sooty mess. Vince's mom brought us each a sandwich and some Kool Aid, which we quickly devoured. Darkness followed the sounds of dinner bells, the chanting of children's names, and the distinctive whistle of the Coady Clan that sounded like a prolonged and deeper Bob White chirp. These were the signals for the children to come home although most of us knew we had better be home with the powering of the streetlights.

Vince and I were not required to come in. His mother had given us a special dispensation for the evening. We stood near one of those streetlights, and Vince asked me for the socks he had requested. I gave him my tube socks and he loaded one with a rock. He explained to me that if I threw it up high, bats would be attracted to it, and he would shoot one. I heaved it up again and again and again—no bats. After twenty minutes of tossing, my arm was very tired. I said, "Vince, you're full of shit." We all loved to swear when we could, "There are no bats." He stoically said, "Keep throwing, you'll see." And I did see. A bat swooped towards the sock. Vince fired and missed. I thought to myself, no one could hit a moving bat; they move too quickly and erratically (except I did not think the word erratically, because it was not yet part of my vocabulary, but I knew what I meant.)

I wish I could say Vince plucked one of those flying rats out of the lamp-lit sky with his next shot, but I cannot, nor did he hit one with the shot after that, or any of the succeeding shots. We continued with our quest until my Dad came to pick me up. My arm was tired; I was dirty; my clothes were covered with wet ashes; my Dad was not happy with my appearance, and yet, I felt a sense of contentment and joy. We had blown up a fire pit, battled our enemy, and nearly killed a moving bat. What a great night!

Chapter Ten

The next day at school Paco approached me at recess. He said, "Sean, look at this bat." He pulled a bat from his pocket—a rubber bat. "I have never seen a rubber bat before." I had seen a rubber bat before, though. My parents had one as part of their costumes for the Halloween party at the Knights of Columbus.

"Where did you get that?" I asked him.

"He was hanging above Sister yesterday. The one I took down."

The sudden realization that Vince lied to me, angered me at first, but then I forgave him and I just knew it was not in Vince's nature to be forthright. Vince had somehow snuck into our classroom and hung that rubber bat above Bony Face's desk before school. I wondered if he had broken in. He probably did. That somehow added to his appeal.

"Paco," I suggested, "Let's not tell anybody, O.K.?"

"I won't say anything. We know who did this don't we?"

He then shrugged and walked away. At that point, that was the most Paco had ever said to me, or anyone else, as far as I knew. Nothing was ever said about the rubber bat, and in Vince's mind his mystique remained untouched.

Chapter Eleven

Of course we were indoctrinated in school. I have already mentioned the number of prayers we were required to say daily, but we also had religion class once a week so we could learn all the Catholic rules-no meat on Friday, no visiting other churches, go to Mass every Sunday and every Holy Day. My favorite Holy Day was the Circumcision which celebrated Christ's briss on January 1st. It was my favorite because my friends and I loved to see all the people with hangovers try to stay awake.

The Nuns would normally teach Religion class, but occasionally Father Nelson himself would teach it. The plethora of prayers and the rules to pray by in the Catholic Church is staggering. Father Nelson shared a list with us that confused, educated, and ultimately entertained us.

He told us about the prayer known as Acts. You had the Act of Faith Prayers that basically worshipped God and thanked him. Then there was the Acts of Contrition which begged forgiveness from God after your *examination of conscious* led one to the obligatory conclusion that you were a worthless, sinning pieces of shit.

The Acts were followed by an explanation of the Cadillac of Prayers the Novena (this prayer is a petition). With this prayer you would ask for something—it was supposed to be something noble like world peace or forgiveness for the Godless communists, but mostly it was for asking for a new bike, a vacation, or a new girlfriend. There was one huge catch to a Novena. **IT WAS A NINE DAY PRAYER!** Rarely did any kid ever finish a Novena. I can't think of one who did.

There was also the granddaddy of all prayers, The Rosary, which is followed by a joyful or sorrowful meditation. In fact, Father Nelson explained that is why it is often chanted by members when prayed aloud, because it is itself a meditation, which relates us dangerously close to the Buddhists.

As you recall, I said we were not only edified in the prayer lesson, but entertained by it too. The last prayer mentioned caused something of a stir. The last prayer covered a short little mindless prayer to be repeated over and over again much like a meditation's mantra. It was designed so one could continuously pray all day as directed by God. The last prayers we learned about was called an Ejaculation. Some of the wiser boys snickered when they heard about this and a short definition of the other meaning of the word made its way around the room for those of us who were unaware. When Father talked about it Jim Beverage raised his hand and asked, with a smirk on his face, "So, Father, an ejaculation is a quick spurt to give us joy in our life?

"Yes, as all prayers are intended." Fathers face was turning red.

Jim kept pushing it, "So, we should have these ejaculations all day long?"

"I already said that." Father was as tense as a caged badger.

"And these ejaculations will get us closer to heaven?"

I swear steam spewed out of Father's balding head, the he shouted "Sister! Come here!!"

Sister Leon rushed over from across the hall. "Yes, Father?"

"Take the girls into your rooms." Father requested.

We all were terrified of Father Nelson, and we were pretty sure he was going to kill Jim Beverage right there, as he didn't want any girls to witness the murder. We were pleasantly surprised when his face relaxed and he told Sister Leon to send in the 5th grade boys.

Vince Agnelneri led the 5th grade boys in because he was the first name alphabetically in his class.

When we had all settled down, Father Nelson said, "It is time some of you boys learned some facts of life." He stared at us over his wire-rimmed glasses. "Jim Beverage thought he was being funny by using a word that has two meanings." He continued, "some of you are not familiar with the other meaning. Soon. very soon, if not already, some of you will have an *occurrence*," he stressed the word occurrence, "in the middle of the night this occurrence may leave you tired or exhilarated. At some point you will feel a sensation in your private area followed by a release, or ejaculation, of bodily fluids which are seeds used to go forth and multiply. This is part of growing up. Just leave it alone. Don't try to make it happen on your own. This is a sin, and some say it will make you go blind. Do you understand?"

In unison we all said "Yes Father".

"Do you have any questions?"

Vince Agnelneri asked, "Father, you said not to make it happen on our own. Can we have someone else make it happen for us like a girl?"

"No, that is an even bigger sin!" Father Nelson boomed.

"Father, is that a venial or mortal sin?" Vince asked.

"A mortal sin. Are there any other questions?"

"Do girls do this to?" asked Jim Beverage.

"No, girls have something else happen to them. What they have to go through is disgusting!" Father replied.

Vince pushed it further when he asked, "What do you call the front part of a girl where she pees?"

I thought I heard Father Nelson whisper "Oh Jesus" under his breath, then he said "Well Vince I'm sure you have a special name for it that you use, but it is called a vagina."

"Oh thank you Father cause I didn't want to use that nasty term for it anymore." Vince's eyes twinkled like Liberace's smoking jacket.

"You are welcome Vince. Are there any other question?" Father Nelson asked, but hoped there was a 'no' reply. He was not so lucky.

Ricky Smart opened up with, "Is it true the Mom has to swallow some seeds to make a baby?"

Father started turning crimson and said, "This is something you need to ask your parents. In fact if you have any more questions, ask them!"

We shuffled out of the room and onto the playground for recess where considerable misinformation about sex was passed around.

Ricky was pretty sure he would soon have a baby brother or sister because he accidently walked in on his parents and it looked like his Mom was swallowing some of his Dad's seeds. Of course Ricky never saw a new baby in the house.

That day was the most fun I ever had learning about prayers.

Chapter Twelve

After the excitements earlier in year were tucked away to the corners of our minds the dreaded monotony of winter class work settled in once again. I had taken to the practice of counting down the seconds until the end of the school day. It was easy, hours times minutes times seconds. We were shut-ins, school-prisoned people. Recess was mostly indoors due to the mostly nasty winter/spring Indiana weather. We did not have a gym, and so our room became our cell. Bony Face gave us busy work drills, and homework that kept us from thinking too hard. With each assignment given, moans and groans returned.

One day in early March Sister Bony Face gave us a homework assignment that proved to be a fatal mistake. It was a dictionary look-up assignment that involved gender. We were to give the feminine equivalent of many words. The list was:

Male...Female

Waiter ...._____

Actor ...._____

Aviator ...._____

Buck..._____

Fox..._____

Bull.._____

Stallion..._____

Hog.._____

This was not too difficult an assignment even for a fourth grader as most of these were common knowledge. The only two, which caused any problem for me, were aviator and fox. So, when working on the assignment at home I asked my sister Evvie for the answers rather than look them up. She was able to give me aviator. "Have you not heard of the famous <u>aviatrix</u>, Amelia Earhart?" She asked. Evvie did not, however, know the female equivalent of fox, and so I was forced to use our ragged-eared dictionary to look it up. I knew better than to ask my parents for the answer as I was aware their answer would be' "Look it up in the dictionary." Webster only gave the definition for fox, noun-a variety of wild dog characterized by etc., etc., etc.

I tried to be creative, foxette, foxes, foxitrix, foxy, ... Then I realized something! A fox is a kind of dog; a female dog is a bitch. Yes! Martha, my English bulldog, my constant companion, shared in my enthusiasm by wagging her tail briskly and sneezing on my leg.

I wished to share my answer with everyone. Bony Face gave us one of those rare opportunities to **grade your own work on the honor system**. I took my paper out and looked at it ready to put the old A on it.

Male...Female

Waiter .... Waitress

Actor .... Actress

Aviator .... Aviatrix

Buck.. Doe

Fox...Bitch

Bull ....Cow

Stallion...Mare

Hog...Sow

Bony Face called out the answers and gave us especially long time to either check them correct or x them wrong. I could see Jim Beverage sliding the stub of a pencil across the page as she called out the correct answers. Jim Beverage was cheating! He had not done his homework. He was writing as she spoke. I was impressed, but angry too. His life was already too easy; he did not have to make it any easier.

Sister droned on: waitress; check, actress; check, aviatrix; check, vixen; x. What? Vixen? Vixen??? With absolutely no forethought, I stood up and yelled aloud,

"No! Sister! Bitch!" The shock wave felt around the room, caused by my eruption, made Vesuvius seem like a popcorn shower. Sister's face turned the color of Lenten service vestments. My mind raced to think of something to distract her from me. In a panic I said, "Jim Beverage was cheating." I pointed at Jim as though she had forgotten whom he was. Jim death-daggered me with his eyes. I returned his stare with a look that said, 'I'm only trying to save myself.'

Bony Face slowly stood up, and slowly crept her way to my side. Her blue-veined, porcelain fingers made an iron claw around her wooden pointer. She beat her other hand with the pointer like a striking teamster would with his tire thumper. She raised that pointer over head like Jesus did when angered by the moneylenders. It made a blaring thunder crush like Joshua's trumpets when it hit my desk. "Sean Raven!" She screamed, which made her normally hawk-like face swell like an overripe plum. "Sean Raven!" she repeated, and then opened her mouth to speak again, but only a church-mouse squeaks came out, "eeeeeek, eeeeek, eek." She dropped her pointer and grabbed her left arm, and then she attempted to sit down on the desk next to me, Paco's desk, but the desk moved as she tried to sit. (I would not swear to it, but I think I saw Paco's hands pulling the desk back as she tried to sit on it.) She fell backward and rocked on her hunched back with her black-laced, high-top, witches' shoes (which I believe were once ruby slippers)pointing to the ceiling, and at the other end of her body her headdress pointed up so that she looked like a human rocker, or a turtle trapped on its back, trying desperately to roll over.

The class set there stunned, paralyzed with fear. After a minute of listening to Sister moan, Marnie Rolls broke our silence and suggested, "Shoont we go ge hep?" I instantly replied, "Are you crazy? She'll get you! She'll grab you if you try to walk past her." At that point I sat down. I looked at Paco Alvarez and he had a slight smile on his face. I smiled back at him. That was an unspoken connection we made.

We watched her rock and moan for some time. Jim Beverage turned to me and lied, "I was not cheating."

"Yes you were."

"No I wasn't"

"I saw you."

"Well. At least I didn't kill Sister Boniface by calling her a bitch."

"I didn't call her a bitch, a female fox is a bitch." I explained. "And besides that she is not dead. She's moaning. She's only pretending." I whispered the last sentence so Sister would not hear me.

"Prove that she is O.K." Jim challenged me.

"How?"

"Help her get up."

All eyes were on me. Peggy Meyer's, the most beautiful girl in the world, eyes were especially beautiful. My logic told me If I could help Sister then Peggy would naturally be impressed. I inched my way towards her, imagining all the while how she might grab me and pull me down beside her. My heart thumped wildly. I could feel everyone's stares. I bent over Sister and whispered to her. "Are you alright?" Had I not know better, I would have said her eyes showed fear, but I knew she was not capable of any emotions except anger, hatred, and arrogance. She did not reply to my question. She did not grab me. She only moaned again softly. At that moment an older student, who was an office helper, walked into the room with a telephone message for someone in the class. When she saw what was happening, she ran out of the room calling for help.

An ambulance came and took her away. She did not die that day, but lived in a hospital, and then a nursing home for almost a year. I believe God gave her an extra year so she could suffer for her sins. We never saw her again. If I should see her in the next life, wherever that may be, then I will explain to her that a fox is a breed of wild dog, and a female dog is a bitch, and so was she.

We had a succession of substitute teachers following Bony Face's departure, and for the first time in our lives we had teachers who were not wearing the black and white statdard habits of nuns. These were normal people without degrees who volunteered for the position. God bless them. We certainly gave them a hard time. It seems when children are suppressed and bullied for a long time, and then suddenly freed from their shackles, they react in one of two ways. One way is they retain their fear and look for another dictatorial leader; they even go so far as to give a leader their permission to be dictatorial. The other way is they go absolutely wild. We went wild. We made Bill Hickock and the man from Borneo look like Peter Cottontail and friend. We disposed of four substitutes in two weeks. We talked loudly: we did not always stand up right away when an adult entered the room; we wrote notes, and passed them; we threw paper wads; we even laughed out loud. Oh my yes, we were wild. We were drunk with defiance. Father Nelson had to come in our room a few times to put the fear of God back into our hearts. Then, at the end of the second week, we were told we would get our permanent replacement from the nunnery of The Sisters of St. John the Divine on the following Monday.

All of us knew there were only two kinds of nuns in the world, and both were of extreme nature. The most common type of nun was like Bony Face, mean spirited, frustrated and bitter. The other type was extremely elusive and rare, seldom seen in public. The other type was like a Hollywood nun-joyful, pretty and kind. Of course we had never met a Hollywood nun, nor had any of our siblings, parents or grandparents; nonetheless, we held a strong hope that our new teacher would be just a movie nun, a happy Ingrid Bergman type with a nice feminine name like Sister Maria, and a gentle demeanor like the mom on the Lassie T.V. show. I'm sure most of us spent the weekend dreaming about what our new nun would be like. All wondering which type of nun would she be.

Chapter Thirteen

That Monday she came. She graced our room with her luminance. Her chubby face glowed golden red framed by the familiar habit. Her smile was stardust. We silently went to our seats and just as silently watched as she erased the substitute's name from the week before off of the chalkboard. She then straightened her desk, and after the bell rang she continued tidying up her area as if nothing had happened. She hummed a tuneless song as she cleaned. We could hear the other rooms chanting their mindless morning prayers. We had the attention span of gnats and her wordless dawdling made us anxious. Some of us started to squirm in our seats. She looked nice, but we knew even at our tender age that looks could indeed be deceiving. She continued to say nothing. She made no eye contact. Ricky Smart coughed and then she finally looked up at us as she stood stone still behind her desk. Her head tilted to one side; her hands were placed in front of her with one palm up and one palm down, fingers lightly touching. She appeared to be posing for a future Holy Card. (For those who are unaware, Holy Cards are like Catholic baseball cards with a saint's likeness on the front and their statistics on the back. (Dragons slain—snakes vanquished—exorcisms performed—gruesomeness of their death, the gorier the better.) At last she spoke, and as she spoke our hearts melted at the sound of her honey-sweet voice. You could tell she was a musical person as her speech was nearly a hymn. She spoke softly, so softly that you almost had to strain to hear her. It was a very effective way to get our attention. What she said did not matter so much as how she said it. She spoke of the future and our potential and rules and expectations. At that moment she could have told us to set our faces on fire and we would have gladly done so. Her name was Sister (believe it or not) Maria. We had finally scored a Hollywood nun. It was heaven on earth. She made learning fun.

There were glorious days for a long while. We had a half hour of music every day with Sister Maria at the once-neglected school piano. My penmanship did not improve, but Sister Maria taught some of the other students and me to print. Curiously, we were never taught to print in first grade, the theory of the day was why waste time teaching children to learn two ways to write when one would suffice. Some of the children learned to print in kindergarten, but since there was no Catholic kindergarten many of our parents declined to put us in public school for that optional grade; therefore, we avoided the evil influence of non-Catholics. We also had art class now, and a kind of P.E. taught by Sister Maria on the playground. She was extremely progressive by teaching us music, art and physical education.

My grades improved along with my attitude, and my behavior was exemplary; consequently, I was named to safety patrol. I was a patrol boy! There were no girls allowed to do such dangerous and manly work. I went through the rigorous one-half hour training program given by Father Nelson for many days, and successfully earned my silver badge on a two-inch, white-webbed canvas shoulder harness. I was the picture of authority. I was only a Safety Patrol Boy in Training, but I did not mind.

The first day on patrol I was stationed at the farthest stop sign from the buses. There was very little traffic there. Vince Agnelneri was my student supervisor. I wondered how my friend ever got picked to be a patrol boy. My cocky large-nosed buddy was not known for his angelic attitude. There was the rumor of his family belonging to the mafia, and they generally got anything they wanted, right? That had to be it.

The first thing he said to me was "They gave you the worst corner." After a long pause he spoke again. "No one can see you here to save you."

"What do you mean save me?"

"The publickers will be coming by soon. They will be looking for revenge." I felt like I was in a John Wayne move, and Vince was warning me about an impending Indian attack.

Just as he predicted, three publickers walked by on the opposite side of the street. One of the three pointed to his elbow, and then he pointed at me. We had a staring contest, and I thought for a moment there would not be a confrontation, but then Vince pulled a small rock from his pocket and hurled it at them yelling "Stinking publickers!"

They turned toward us, produced and threw their rocks at us and yelled back with "Catlickers!" They threw as they ran and then scurried off down the street. It was a short and sweet battle.

"I'd say we won that one." Vince bleated. "So, you know what to do?"

"Yes," I replied. "I give a hand signal to stop all traffic then stand three feet off the curb and motion the students to cross."

"Not that, dumb-ass." He bleated again. "Always carry rocks in your pocket to throw at the publickers. I won't always be here to defend you."

"Oh yeah, I got it, and I can handle myself." I lied.

There were no pedestrians that day to assist across the street, nor the following days which were spent with Vince Agnelneri. Of course the three publickers returned regularly and we carried on our rock throwing ritual each day.

The following week I was to patrol alone for the first time. I felt only a little anxious about facing those kids alone. The battles had been, so far, almost friendly exchanges, None of us had hit anyone yet.

Chapter Fourteen

The weatherman will tell you the hottest day of the year in Indiana is near the end of July, and technically he would be correct; however, the hottest day comes in late March or April or May when the morning starts out brisk and chilly and you wear a sweater, or your favorite plastic sailor coat with anchors for decorations, and it is quite comfortable on the way to school or work, but when it comes time to go home the sun has played its springtime game of hot potato and you are soon baking like that same unwanted spud.

The hottest day in 1963 came in April. It was brisk in the morning, warm at lunchtime, and hot enough at afternoon recess to strip down to your t-shirt. By dismissal time the un-air conditioned classroom was stiflingly hot and stuffy. Not even Sister Maria's sweet smile could cool us.

Immediately after school I made my way to my appointed corner wearing my canvas safety-patrol belt over my red sweater, and my sailor coat hung loosely in my right hand which I dragged on the sidewalk as I plodded along. I laid my coat on the grass and attended my patrol duties.

That day I actually escorted a person across the street. He was an elderly man (I knew he had to be at least 50 years old.) It was a glorious moment. I walked out three feet, held my arms out, and motioned him on. He even said, "Good job, kid." His being there caught me off guard for the publickers sneak attack. As I was walking back to my post, ever so proud of myself, a dime-sized piece of gravel smacked my earlobe. The publickers were on my side of the street! This was truly a violation of the articles of war, and it scared the shit out of me!

I instinctively reached for my rocks, but they were in my beautiful sailor coat pocket which lay three feet away on the ground. I was defenseless, and the Protestants knew it. The biggest publicker, although he was smaller than me, asked, "What's the matter catlicker? Cat got your tongue? What, ain't you got no cat guts, or are they all wasted on your violin? You pussy!" The three of them started inching closer and I backed up in pace with them. Then they suddenly burst at me, spraying me with rocks as they ran past me, laughing. The laughing was definitely more painful than the pelting with the stones. I could have used a savior then, and luckily one came by in the shape of a big yellow bus. Father Nelson was driving and he swerved dangerously close to the publickers and me. They scattered when they saw the expression on Father Nelson's face.

I quickly got on the bus and sat next to Vince Agnelneri. He looked at me and said, "Your ear is bleeding."

"Yeah," I replied in the manliest voice I could muster, "The publickers got me."

"Cool, you've got your red badge of courage."

"What?" I did not know what 'the red badge of courage' meant then, and Vince did not want me to think he actually read anything.

"Forget it." He said, "That is just cool."

Vince Agnelneri thought I was cool. I swelled with pride. That was the best compliment he ever gave me.

We were about halfway through the bus route when my elation turned to terror. I was taking off my safety belt, and I was going to put it in my coat pocket when I realized I had left the coat on the sidewalk. My stomach churned with the anticipation of the response I would get from my parents. My Dad would lecture on responsibility. My mother would cry pitifully, and she would probably be unable to carry on with daily life. The emotions roiled within me so that I began to rock back and forth in my seat. Vince gave me a sideways glance and bleated, "Knock it off!" which I did immediately. So in a few brief moments I had gone from super cool, fighting catlicker, to a whimpering loser. I knew at that moment I would never amount to anything. My life was bound to be a complete waste of time and energy.

When I got home I raced up to my room in an effort to avoid Mom. With any luck she would not notice I was coatless. But of course she would notice. She yelled at me every day about hanging my coat up in my bedroom closet. I zipped up the stairs and made a production of opening the closet door, ruffling the other clothes and hangars and closing the door loudly. Then I walked into the kitchen and said, "Hi Mom," I said it with a little too much volume for she looked at me suspiciously, but she only said, "Well, hi Sean. How was school?"

"Fine." I fibbed

She had a look of concern and asked, "What happened to your ear?"

"Umm, I bumped my head on the bus window. You know how I told you Father Nelson gets crazy when he drives the school bus." I was becoming quite the accomplished liar.

"Maybe I should have a talk with Father Nelson. He needs to be more careful."

"No, no don't do that, Mom, it's not a big deal."

"O.K., but let's clean that off." She opened the medicine cabinet above the bathroom sink and brought out the dreaded isopropyl rubbing alcohol. She was a fiend with that tortuous liquid. She would drown any wound with it. She pushed my head over the sink and rinsed off the earlobe. She poured half a bottle on the cut. The initial sting caused me to jerk up and bang my temple on the faucet. Her cure was going to kill me. I let out a yelp that sounded like the time I accidentally stepped on Martha's paw. I was more than willing to suffer through this ordeal because this distraction kept her from noticing my lack of a coat.

I did not sleep well that night and I planned to search the street corner in the morning for my precious coat. I begged my parents to let me ride my bicycle to school the next day so I could get there early and start looking for the coat. Dad was all for it, but Mom had reservations. The discussed it in front of me.

"The boy needs the exercise." Dad started. "Maybe he could lose some of that fat on him." (Thanks Dad)

"But Daddy, he could get hit." My Mom said nervously with her hand to her mouth.

"How could any driver not see his fat ass?" (Appreciate it, Dad.)

Mom turned to me and quietly asked, "You'll be careful, won't you?" She hugged me ferociously.

The next morning I pedaled my fat ass the two miles to school, easily beating the bus. I parked my fat-tired Schwinn in the school's rusted iron bike rack and ran to my patrol post. There was nothing but empty sidewalk on the corner. Nothing down the street could be seen. I walked by the nuns' house, which was next to the school, and what I saw made my heart skip a beat. Sister Maria was standing at the back door holding my coat up with outstretched arms, but below the coat was a pair of short legs with rolled-up cuffed blue jeans. She put the coat on the child and spun him around. It was Paco Alvarez! My first instinct was to shout, but something kept me from making any noise. I wanted to scream, "The Lord giveth and the Lord taketh away" but I did not. I thought of Paco's tear laden face the day we found out mine was the only gift he received for Christmas, and how I short-changed him with that balsa wood glider. Sister Maria smiled and hugged him. At that moment his father, a larger copy of Paco, took his hand and led him to an old pick-up truck. They left that day for better opportunities elsewhere. As that rust bucket pulled away I yelled, "Merry Christmas Paco Alvarez!"

Later

·—————•❦•—————·

There was no Catholic High School in our small city so after eighth grade our class split up and we went to various institutions. Some of the girls, including Marnie Rolls, elected to go to the girls' catholic boarding school, St. Margaret's Academy for Young Ladies, which was only 25 miles away. Jim Beverage commuted with two upperclassmen all the way to Indianapolis to the all-boys Jesuit High School. Three of our classmates lived on farms, and they all attended the county school just east of our town. The rest of us went to the city high school with our sworn enemies the publickers (for the most part, we became good friends with the publickers). Some of us flourished in the public school system, others floundered.

Public high school was an adjustment for me, and despite repeated warnings from my sister, and

Vince Agnelneri, I still stood up from force of habit the first time an adult walked into our classroom. This resulted in some snickers and the epithet stupid catlicker. I managed to survive that barrage and I was one of the fortunate few who flourished in the relatively freedom-filled halls of public high school. Ricky Smart did not fare so well. He skipped school as often as he attended and shortly after his sixteenth birthday he simply stopped coming to school, back when quitting school was not so carefully scrutinized. Ricky worked menial jobs for several years. He lived at home until his mom and dad died in a fire, and then he moved on to homeless shelters and old cars. Fortunately for Ricky, Jim Beverage chanced upon him one day and hired him on the spot to work at The Beverage Chain Link Fence Co. Ricky bought a doublewide trailer and he lives in it to this day at Possum Trot Trailer Park. He lives there with his wife. His two children and three grandchildren occasionally visit or find refuge there in trying times. He continues to do custodial chores at Jim's company.

I have learned not to be jealous of Jim Beverage, although he has led a charmed life. Jim had a great time in high school, and he was social chairman of his fraternity in college. Shortly after his schooling he went to work, obviously, at his family's business. Jim managed the business well and he steadily increased sales and production. He married a beauty queen (Miss Pork Festival of Tilton County) they met in college and have three charming and beautiful daughters.

After Marnie Rolls graduated from the academy she entered a convent. She earned top grades and became a humble and model novice nun. The order she joined is very devout, strict, and reclusive. They are known as the Impoverished Sisters of St. Anna. I understand that Marnie took a vow of silence, removed her hearing aids and has yet to put them back in after some thirty or more years of quiet solitude and meditation. I must admire this strange choice she made.

My sister Evvie became a special education teacher. She remains married to a cousin of the farmer who sold us Martha, the English bulldog. She has become quite an accomplished artist and has sold several of her paintings. She still lives in our city.

Vince Agnelneri continued to instruct me in the ways (many of which are wayward ways) of the world throughout high school. The night of his graduation he burned down his neighbor's garage by mismanaging some illegal fireworks. He was caught, tried, and given the choice: jail, or the army. He should have chosen jail. I learned of his death a year later from our newspaper. "Local Hero Killed in Vietnam" the headline read. I still miss my criminal mentor.

Peggy Meyers, the most beautiful girl in the world, remained beautiful, sweet, charming, and successful and out of my reach throughout high school. She once gave me a ride home after school. We stopped for a cola and talked about grade school, high school, and the future. She confessed to me that she wanted to be an actress, and after college she left for California. If you ever get a chance to see a movie called Civil War II she plays the governor's wife, Cassandra. I am sure you will agree with me that she is the most beautiful girl in the world. Nowadays Peggy lives in a suburb of Chicago with her pediatrician husband, and she regularly acts in local theater productions.

As for me I've already told you I have had a couple of wives. I left the church of course, since it frowns upon twice-married sinners. I have five wonderful mostly-grown children, and I am still married to wife number two. I attempted to major in business administration in college, but I could not get past the required math, so I followed in my sister's footsteps and I became a teacher.

I now live and teach in Indianapolis. The other day, my wife and I were cleaning out closets of our nearly empty nest. She suggested (and when I say suggested, I mean demanded) that I take some of the children's outgrown coats to the Catholic Charities as it was having its annual drive for coats for kids. She also suggested (and by suggested I of course mean demanded) that I have them dry-cleaned first; which I did. Being the procrastinator that I am I was a day late for any of the many the drop-off location, so I had to take the coats to the Catholic Charities main office in downtown Indy.

The office was neat and tidy with many plaques and awards on the walls. A secretary's desk shielded the director's office, but his door was open and something caught my eye. Above and behind the director's desk in a cherry wood shadow box a small child's coat was displayed. It had white anchors in a field of navy blue. The coat was plastic. The nameplate on the desk read "P. Alvarez." In the chair behind the desk sat a much heavier much older Hispanic gentleman. He looked up from his computer and stared at me for a moment. He then looked down, then back up at me, smiled broadly and finally responded to my greeting all those years earlier and said, "Merry Christmas Sean Raven!"

From the Author

————•●⚞●•————

This novella has been a labor of love for me, and just like love; it has had its ups and downs. Many of those who have read Pace Alvarez ask me if Sean Raven is actually me. They want to know if any of the incidents in the story are true. Did I really poop my pants? Did I kill a nun? Did we explode a trash can with gasoline? Was there a bat, real or fake, living in my classroom? Well, thanks to an army of lawyers waiting to pounce on any opportunity to sue someone, I am obligated to say everything in this story is fictional. I also have a few people to thank.

I am a child of the fifties and sixties, so, like many of my contemporaries, the learning curve for computer and other technological devices has been slow and painful. It took me forever to type this novella. I originally wrote it out by hand on lunch hours and breaks, and sometimes when

I should have been working (thanks unwitting employers). The current youthful generation does not understand that a male of my generation never learned to type unless he was preparing to go in the army, or was afraid he would be drafted. The reason behind this was a clerk in the army was less likely to be involved with deadly military action. I did take a typing class in high school, but never used that skill after the class. I had a high lottery number so I did not fear going to Vietnam. My generation of males paid others (women, of course {those who were not pregnant, barefoot and in the kitchen where they belong} made money this way) to type for them in college. When I finally joined the twentieth century and started to type on a computer I pounded the hell out of the keys expecting them to react much the same way as the Smith Corona manual typewriter keys once did. The light touch of a laptop is way too sensitive for me, and I find myself landing in the strangest places just by accidentally touching an area where an ad has been placed. Someone should make a computer for those of us with a heavier touch. I, as usual, digress too much. What I want to say is I have had one mishap after another with the copy of this story. I packed it away on old computer before I was convinced to publish it. When Peggy (my wife) dragged it out of storage and copied to a flash drive then e-mailed it back to me; it somehow ended up garbled and nonsensical, fortunately I had an extra hard copy, and even more fortunately, my lovely wife retyped the whole thing, again extra, extra, fortunately she was not barefoot, pregnant, and in the kitchen.

Did I say everything in Merry Christmas Paco Alvarez was fictional? Well, not exactly everything. There are many historical allusions which are true. The Palmer Method to better penmanship existed. Many things were similar in my life. I do have terrible handwriting. I did accidentally kill a nun when she lost her temper with me. I didn't mean to; it just happened. I had an Italian friend who taught me to shoot matches from a BB gun. Most importantly I did have a beautiful plastic coat with anchor decorations covering it. I don't know why that coat was so precious to me, but I can still picture it perfectly in my mind.

As I said, I have a few people to thank for their assistance. I need to thank those who read the early draft and encouraged me, especially my sisters, brother, and my wife. I also need to thank Sally Hoffman and Jack Beattie for editing the book. I am so glad you are both sticklers. The beautiful cover art is thanks to my talented son-in-law, Rick Poplin. I hope those of you who read it enjoyed the book. Thanks everyone!

John Raab